No rules.

No honor.

No quarter.

THE AGENT. Sophisticated, cunning, ruthless. His hands are clean, because others do his dirty work. His conscience is clear, because other peoples' lives don't matter.

THE FALL GUY. Tough, decent, deadly. He was loyal to the CIA, until they betrayed him. He was a private citizen, until they declared war. He was the victim—until he got revenge.

THE WOMAN. Beautiful, loving, vulnerable. She never suspected her lover's past. Until they caught her alone...and used her to teach him a brutal lesson.

WAR TOYS

HAMPTON HOWARD

AVON
PUBLISHERS OF BARD, CAMELOT, DISCUS AND FLARE BOOKS

AVON BOOKS
A division of
The Hearst Corporation
1790 Broadway
New York, New York 10019

The Stein and Day, Inc. edition contains the following Library of
Congress Cataloging in Publication Data:

Howard, Hampton.
  War toys.

  I. Title.
PS3558.O8817W3   1983   813'.54   82-40008

First Avon Printing, February, 1984

For Lady

ONE

Although THE POLICE never asked her to aid them in their inquiries—indeed, never *made* any inquiries as far as she could tell—it was, nonetheless, Madame Bob Jiji, trained as a laundress in the Senegal and employed as a dispenser of change in the self-service laundry in the rue des Blancs-Manteaux, who most clearly saw the incident that evening.

She had first noticed the men as they emerged from a parked car immediately across from the Laundromat.

Madame Bob Jiji took considerable professional pride in her ability to assign occupation accurately on the basis of dress. The blue track suit with the red stripe, she quickly decided, was a mechanic, perhaps a handyman. The coarse wool suit, with what Madame Bob Jiji instantly and censoriously recognized as a clip-on tie, puzzled her for a moment, until a glance at the face, at the bully's arrogance of eyes and mouth, enabled her to identify him as a Colonial Administrator.

The third man, an Algerian dressed in soiled *bleu de travail* and actually carrying his broom, required no such exercise of imagination, although later Madame Bob Jiji was to reflect on the phenomenon, unique to her experience, of a chauffered streetsweeper.

Madame Bob Jiji was here briefly distracted from her speculations by a request for change, and when she returned to her observation post at the door she saw, with utter clarity and complete astonishment, that the three men were about to attack a banker.

The Banker—expensive gray suit, thin stripe, English wool or Madame Bob Jiji missed her guess—was oblivious to the ominous triangulation of which he was the focus. Before him the Mechanic approached from the shop of Antoine, the cobbler. Behind him, the Colonial Administrator emerged from the door of the *Vin Nicolas,* closing fast. Across the street, in a particularly authenticating touch, the sweeper leaned on his broom, motionless.

As the Banker, tall and fair-haired, came abreast of the Mechanic, the Mechanic stepped into his path and raised his hand, greeting him, it seemed, by name. In response, the Banker, with a speed Madame Bob Jiji could not follow, struck him squarely in the face, sending him flying backward into the outdoor display of the *marchand de couleurs* next door, where he lay in a tangle of shopping bags, dusters, shoe polish, and floor wax. *"Starwax,"* Madame Bob Jiji noticed helplessly—*"La cire qui glace!"*

When she looked back again, the Colonial Administrator was on the ground, wrapped tightly about his groin, and the Algerian lay motionless part way beneath a blue Renault, his toes turned inward, oddly rigid, an open springlock knife still in his hand.

The Banker, impossibly, was gone.

After a moment, the Colonial Administrator pushed himself to a sitting position with one arm, vomited quietly into his lap, and, just before he fainted, said, "Oh, la *la*...," sounding, Madame

4

Bob Jiji would have told the police had they ever asked, just like Maurice Chevalier in *Fanny*.

Archivists rarely agree on the precise origin of a case history. For one, the rude disruption of Madame Bob Jiji's afternoon had its genesis in a minor intelligence scandal in the Balkans four years prior. Another might argue with equal strength that the case truly began only three years earlier, with the unsolved murder of a Yugoslav journalist in the rue Quincampoix.

From a strictly operational standpoint, however—first meeting on French soil—it had begun the previous month in a small hotel in Paris.

TWO

THE HOTEL WAS on the very edge of the Seventeenth arrondissement, overlooking the Porte de Champerret.

The smell of *choucroute* from an Alsatian brasserie on the ground floor filled the small and sparsely furnished room in which the two men sat.

The elder of the two, silver-haired and expensively dressed, spoke slowly.

"What does 'not active' mean?" he asked. "He likes chess? He's got mono?"

The other man was solidly built, in his late forties. His face was tan, his blond hair crew-cut, and the steadiness of his voice, when he replied, emphasized rather than masked the effort of control he brought to his speech.

"It means he was terminated three years ago, Mr. Burnham," the man said tightly. "The file doesn't indicate anything about chess or mono."

"Why was he terminated?" Burnham asked.

"It's all in the file," the crew-cut man snapped.

"I haven't read the file," Winthrop Burnham said pleasantly, crossing his legs. "Why don't you fill me in? I'd be interested in an Operations interpretation."

The crew-cut man lit an unfiltered cigarette and looked around for an ashtray. Seeing none, he lifted the edge of the bedspread and flipped the dead match beneath the bed on which he sat. He then picked a shred of tobacco from the tip of his tongue, which he examined carefully as he spoke.

"Mr. Burnham," he said slowly, "let me review my marching orders with you, all right? Just the way Blaine gave them to me this morning." He began to count on his fingers. "I am, repeat *am*, to pull a wire copy of Fredericks's 201 from Central Registry. I *am* to proceed to the far reaches of the 17th where, at a prearranged time and place, i.e., here and now, I *am* to turn that file over to one Winthrop Burnham, even though his name is conspicuous by its absence on a *very* short subscription list. I am *not* to file a contact report, on authority of Head of Station, and I am *not,* repeat *not,* to notice that even though it's a dead file it's carrying a current diagraph for Western Europe."

The man paused. "I think that's it, Mr. Burnham," he said. "There's nothing at all there about interpretations."

"Are you going to tell me what happened?" Burnham asked.

There was a long moment before the crew-cut man spoke.

"Sure," he said finally. "He was running a network in Belgrade and the Vojvodina. It turned out there was a bad apple. The network got rolled up, some people got shot, Fredericks had to leave in his socks."

"So what's the big problem?" Burnham asked. "Those things happen, surely it's part of the game?"

From the restaurant below a sudden roar of laughter rose to them from a table of traveling salesmen dawdling over their post-luncheon coffee and cognac. When the laughter died, there was only the sound of the afternoon traffic on the Boulevard Peripherique.

"That's just the problem, Mr. Burnham," the crew-cut man said, his anger now evident. "He failed entirely to see it as a game. He just couldn't get his perspective right. He kept on thinking about dead agents and got mad. He couldn't stop thinking about his bad apple, either..."

"That's not what I meant..." Burnham began, but the crew-cut man was speaking fast now, determined to be done.

"Now as I understand it, Mr. Burnham, which is admittedly not very damned much, your operations background is a little thin. Let me help you here. Agents are dependents, Mr. Burnham, sorta like kids. They are *tough* to forget, when something happens to them. What happened to Fredericks could happen to *any* case officer decent enough—dumb enough, if you prefer—to care about his people. It's every professional's nightmare. What usually happens is something simple, like, say, you can't stop crying. Fredericks decided to play catch-up instead, and even though I don't know him, I'm pretty sure I'd rather stay awake for a week than have one of his nights."

The crew-cut man stopped, breathed deeply, and crossed to the open window. He flipped the butt of his cigarette into the courtyard and lit another.

"Will he do us a favor if we ask right?" Burnham asked.

"Leave him alone," the crew-cut man said dully, not turning.

"What does he do?"

"He's self-employed. Software consulting. Read the goddamned file and surveillance reports."

"How do I get in touch with him?" Burnham asked.

The younger man rose from the bed, buttoned his overcoat, and crossed to the door. "Well, Mr. Burnham," he said, "this's outside my brief, but

11

I'll tell you what I'd do. I'd use the phone. It's fast, it's cheap, and it works at least half the time. If nobody answers, I'd leave a message with *Abonnés Absents,* ask him to call me back. That's what I'd do."

The crew-cut man was at the door when Burnham spoke.

"What happened to his bad apple?" he asked, almost as an afterthought.

The man turned and regarded Burnham.

"That's in the file, too, Mr. Burnham," he said, "but on this one I'll save you the reading time. They had to pick that son of a bitch up with a spoon is what happened to him. You might want to keep that in mind when you're making Fredericks's plans for him."

The door closed behind him, hard.

After a few minutes the white-haired man rose and walked to the bed.

He picked up the string-tied file folder that the other man had left for him.

The tab read: *FREDERICKS, N.M.*

The folder seemed very thin to carry the classification that it did.

Burnham untied the file and withdrew a five-by-eight file photo clipped to the top page. This he perused for a long moment before returning it to the file.

He then put the file into his briefcase, picked up his coat, turned out the light, and left, reflecting on the odd incongruity, given the contents of the file, that its subject looked just like a banker.

THREE

By THE BEGINNING of the seventeenth century, that area of Paris known as the Marais—for the swamp lying to either side of the (then) raised rue Saint-Antoine which had been cleared and settled by monks and Templars three centuries prior—had become the fashionable hub of the city, home to the nobility and attendants of the Bourbon court.

Its glorious day, alas, was short. With the building of the place Vendôme, the Faubourg Saint-Germain, and the Invalides, the nobility moved west; the fall of the Bastille antedated the fall of the Marais from fashion by but a few years.

The apartment of the woman with whom Noah Fredericks had lived for the past three years consisted of the upper two floors of an ancient and mansarded *hôtel particulier* surviving, barely, from that period.

Protected as an historical monument by the Malraux Law of 1962, its enemy now was merely time, not man. Its west wall canted perilously above the narrow rue Vielle du Temple, buttressed against collapse by massive, hoary wooden girders. Had the wall fallen during its construction, the debris would have littered the courtyard and disturbed the day of the playwright Beaumarchais who had, then, recently completed *The Barber of Seville* and was at work on *The Marriage of Figaro*.

The vague thought of its collapse, now, troubled

only the sleep of the Algerian and Jewish mothers of the quarter, whose children, in the day among its shadows, played those games and told those stories possible only in wooden forts of great antiquity.

It was well past the dinner hour, the soft dusk of Paris April deepening to blue, as Fredericks, walking, turned into the narrow, quiet street that evening.

He was a large man, fair-haired, with thick, sloping shoulders and an athlete's easy gait. He was walking fast. In the dying light, the four small Arab boys playing soccer at the mouth of the rue des Ecouffes down the street noticed him only as he paused before the entranceway to the building.

Occasionally during the past year, on evenings of clear weather and gentle mood, Fredericks would pause and play with the boys, goal tending in the mouth of the alley, three shots out of five behind him winning a franc.

Although two out of five never won the franc, a rule strictly respected, such exceptional considerations as truly atrocious luck or particularly short legs not infrequently resulted in the awarding of a penalty shot.

As the boys called to him through the dusk that evening, however, Fredericks did not respond.

"Quatre sur cinq!" shouted one of the boys hopefully, but even such a gross revision of the odds in his favor failed that evening to tempt him, or even, surprisingly, to elicit a wave. Instead, as the boys watched, riveted, Fredericks put his foot to the heavy wooden door and shoved, hard. The door slammed inward, and Fredericks, entering behind it with a speed not previously demonstrated in goal, was gone as suddenly as he had appeared.

"Pissed off!" said one of the boys, with some awe.

"Drunk," asserted the littlest, firmly.

"Mais non," said Yousef, the eldest and thus most privy to the trials of men. *"C'est le foutu boulot."*

The fucking job.

Fredericks pressed the glowing button just inside the entranceway.

The lights that illuminated the entrance hall and stairwell went on with a soft thud.

No one.

Although he could feel the wet weight of his sleeve against his arm, only a small stain showed at his shoulder, hardly noticeable against the dark fabric of his suit coat.

Moving quickly, he closed the outside door firmly behind him, propping the aluminum lid of a nearby garbage can against it, and crossed to the stairs.

On the second landing the shaking forced him to stop for a moment. Just shock, he reminded himself, leaning quietly against the wall and breathing deeply and deliberately as the landing light winked out.

In the warm dark he could smell garlic, onions, and frying potatoes. Listening carefully, the only sounds he could hear were postdinner family voices and, somewhere, a television.

They did not want money, he thought.

The stairwell was quite silent.

They knew my name, he thought.

In the dim light that filtered into the stairwell from a small window giving onto an airshaft, the thin tongue of the switchblade knife that Fredericks held in his right hand, and which, three minutes before, he had driven into the side of a stranger's head, glinted dully.

Fredericks thumbed back the spring lock on the knife and the blade sagged. He squeezed gently, locking it with a soft click into the dark handle, and replaced it in his right suit-coat pocket.

Outside the door of their apartment he paused again, listening.

He heard Danielle's low laugh and recognized the rapid, affected, anecdotal voice of Lucien, her hairdresser at Alexandre and primary confidant in matters of professional gossip.

Fredericks entered, closing and locking the door behind him.

Danielle and Lucien were at the far end of the low living room, relaxed in armchairs by the fire.

Danielle rose and came toward Fredericks on long legs, her mass of tawny hair illuminated by the light of the fire behind her.

"Bon soir, chéri," she said, smiling happily. "Lucien just stopped by for a glass. He says he wants to cut and curl me for the Lanvin show, can you imagine it?"

"Salut, patron!" called Lucien from his chair. "You're late. Working hard?"

"An old French tradition, Luke," Fredericks called with seeming *bonhomie* from the door. "The hairdressers knock off at five and hair-splitters stay till six. Damned if I know why."

Lucien laughed. "Listen, will you please tell her that you'll still love her with short hair? She won't believe me."

Such assurances, however, were not immediately forthcoming, for even as Lucien spoke Fredericks had turned and was ascending the small spiral staircase that led to their bedroom and bath above.

"*Ça va, cheri?*" Danielle asked anxiously. "*Tu vas bien?*"

"Get him out," Fredericks said softly, not turning his head.

At the top of the stairs Fredericks breathed deeply and raggedly, then peeled off his suit coat. The silk lining of the left sleeve, which stuck wetly to his arm and turned inside-out as he removed it, was sodden with blood. His shirt sleeve was crimson from shoulder to wrist, and in the cool night air he could feel the wetness on his back.

Below, Fredericks could hear the jangling of bracelets as Lucien put on his coat and purred his goodbyes.

"*...you* know, my dear, the enormous one with the horrible claws. *It* comes from North America, too. *Grubby* bear, is it?"

"That's *grizzly* bear, Lucien, and don't be naughty. Call me tomorrow. I'll be at Fath all afternoon."

In the bathroom, Fredericks stripped to the waist, tossing the blood-soaked shirt into the tub. Two blue golf-ball-sized swellings, one in the middle of his left forearm and another in the thick muscle of his left shoulder, stood out lividly against his fair skin, the small obscene mouths in the center of each still seeping blood.

He could not see the one in his back, beneath the left shoulder blade. Hoping that it was only the wound's stiffening that pained him to breathe, Fredericks bent over the sink, breathed deeply, coughed, and spat.

The spittle was clear.

Fredericks heard the door closing below and

then the clinking of ice cubes being dropped into a glass.

"Well, at least you didn't call him Luke the Barber," sighed Danielle as she came up the stairs bringing him a whisky. "Of course, now he thinks we're so hopelessly depraved that we'll be going at it like teenagers before he reaches the street. Which, come to think of it, if you'd hurry a bit...my God! Oh, my God! Your back! What happened!?"

"I don't know yet," Fredericks said without turning, breathing deeply and spitting again. "Put it on the table."

"Oh my God," she whispered, sloshing whisky onto the glass top of her makeup table. "What happened? What's in there?"

"Nothing," Fredericks said in a chillingly conversational tone. "Stab wounds always come up quickly."

"Stab?" Her hands flew to her mouth, her fingers digging white into her cheeks, as she saw the two livid wounds on the front of Fredericks's body.

Fredericks reached past her and picked up the whisky from the table.

He drained the glass in three, long swallows, then emptied the ice into a washcloth, which he held in his left hand, twisting it tightly into a bag.

He held the glass out to Danielle.

"Would you get me some more ice?" he asked, with terrifying courtesy.

Danielle, panting harshly through her hands, was unable to move her gaze from the grotesque blue ball of bruise at his shoulder.

"Noah...my God...what happened?"

"Ice," Fredericks reminded her gently, with an encouraging smile that, when she raised her eyes and saw it, chilled her still more horribly, for there was nothing in it of his smile, and it made his face not his.

Unable to move or to take her eyes from him, Danielle could clearly hear, as though in some way amplified, the dripping of water in the bathroom sink, the ticking of the clock beside their bed, the sound of the television of the Arab family across the narrow street, and, three floors below, the clatter of an aluminum garbage can cover on the stones of the entranceway.

Then Fredericks had her by the arm and was speaking softly, though urgently and in English, as he seated her on the edge of the bed and placed the telephone in her lap.

"Listen, Dany, call the police. Tell them to come right away. The address, top floor. O.K.?"

As he finished speaking, Fredericks heard from the stairwell below a terrified and indignant squawk, suddenly and brutally truncated in mid-breath. Wrong time, wrong place, Lucien, thought Fredericks. That's what you get for dyeing it blond, you silly shit.

"Noah..." Danielle whispered, her large eyes wide and spilling tears of fear and confusion.

"Baby, do it," Fredericks said. "Get the operator. Now."

Heavy feet could be heard on the stairwell, taking no care to muffle their approach. Too many of them, Fredericks thought briefly, and then there was thunderous pounding on the door and a heavy voice was shouting, *"Police judiciaire! Ouvrez!!"*

"They're already here!" Danielle whispered, her face flooded with relief and incredulity. That they should have arrived without being summoned was, for Danielle in her shock, no source of disquiet but rather the simple manifestation of a benign and prescient Providence.

To Fredericks it made all the difference in the world.

"Son of a bitch," he softly breathed. "Son of a *bitch*."

Fredericks knelt quickly, fished the knife from the pocket of his ruined suit coat, and crossed to the open bedroom window. The silent street below was spectrally lit with flashing blue lights. They were there, all right.

With a sharp snap of the wrist, Fredericks flipped the knife into the darkness over the sloping roof of the building across the narrow street and turned to Danielle.

"Noah...?" she said.

The pounding on the door was more insistent now, and the heavy voice continued to shout, "Police! The door!"

Fredericks knelt before Danielle and gently held her face in his square, thick fingers.

"Dany, listen," he said softly, "they'll tell you things that you won't want to hear, but they're only true if you believe them, *tu comprends?*"

Danielle began to weep.

Someone was beating the door now with an open hand, and a second voice had begun to shout, "Open it!"

Fredericks lifted Danielle's chin with his forefinger and held her flooded eyes with his.

"Dany... he began, then stopped. "Baby, you stay up here," he caressed her cheek, stood, turned, and was gone.

From the head of the stairs, and in her dreams for weeks to come, Danielle could see and hear everything that happened next, quite clearly.

At the front door Fredericks paused, looked carefully around him, then slipped the lock and stepped quickly back.

The door erupted inwards.

The first policeman through, a heavy-set uniformed foot patrolman, hesitated for a moment as his eyes found Fredericks and then, cursing, swung at Fredericks's head with a black rubber and steel *matraque*.

As he swung, Fredericks stepped inside the arc of the club and struck the policeman a short chopping blow to the throat.

At thirty-four, Noah Fredericks stood a bit over six feet and weighed two hundred pounds, of which only four or five were fat. The blow was of enormous force, and hurled the heavy-set policeman like a child against the side of the refrigerator where he collapsed in a clatter of rolling bottles and broken crockery, as Danielle screamed.

Fredericks turned back to the door. Two uniformed policemen, one standing and one kneeling, held shotguns pointed squarely at his chest. A third aimed an automatic pistol with both hands at arms' length, not six feet from Fredericks's head.

Behind them were more policemen, and an older, dark-haired man in civilian clothes. It was the man in the suit who spoke.

"Right there, my friend," he said, in the flat accent of the North. "The bag limit on cops is one a day, and you've already got two."

For a long moment of clenched silence, no one moved.

And then, the flat glare fading from his eyes, Fredericks slowly raised his hands and placed them on his head, as the police for whom he had not called, and a past that he had always known would one day call again for him, came through the door and took him.

It was three weeks to the day since his lunch with Winthrop Burnham.

FOUR

IT WAS A sunny Sunday morning, so the chroniclers record, the twenty first of January 1793, when the blade of the guillotine flashed and fell in the Square of the Revolution, spattering the block straw with the mortal residue of King Louis XVI.

Two years later, with the blood of the more than thirteen hundred who were to follow him still stiffening in the mire near the Tuileries gate, the Directory, manifesting an appalling facility for public relations, renamed the square, Concorde.

Today as then, the place de la Concorde is dominated from the north by two imposing mansions in the style of Louis XV, seated on either side of the opening to the rue Royale.

The right pavilion, originally the royal furniture store, now houses the Office of the Admiralty.

That to the left, first occupied by four noblemen, is today shared by the Hôtel Crillon and the Automobile Club of France, where, three weeks earlier, Fredericks had been invited to lunch.

Save the name the man had offered on the telephone, Fredericks knew, that day, only one thing about his host.

The man was a liar.

The dining room of the Automobile Club commands an imposing view, and thus Fredericks, having given the name of his host to the captain, was pleased to find himself led to a window table.

As they approached, a white-haired gentleman, dressed and groomed with a loving elegance quite consonant with that of the room, rose and smiled a tentative welcome over his half-glasses.

"Mr. Fredericks?" he said.

"Yes," Fredericks said. The man's hand, soft and thin and dry, disappeared briefly as Fredericks took it.

"Winthrop Burnham," the man said. "I'm delighted that you could come. Won't you sit down?"

Fredericks did so.

"A drink, Mr. Fredericks?"

"Please. A *pastis*."

"And an American martini," Burnham said without turning, as the captain bowed and withdrew.

"Well, Mr. Fredericks," Burnham said, settling himself and lighting a cigarette, "as I mentioned to you on the telephone, I am with Jobert Frères."

Jobert Frères was the most powerful and prestigious American law firm in Paris.

Fredericks nodded pleasantly.

"Several days ago, Mr. Fredericks, I had occasion to lunch with Jacques Rondet of Crédit Lyonnais, and when I mentioned that we were looking for an American consultant with experience in French finance, your name came up."

"Really?" Fredericks smiled slightly.

"He was most complimentary," Burnham said, smiling back.

"Mr. Burnham," Fredericks said affably, "I'm currently doing a little consulting job for their trading division, adding some largely regulatory whistles and bells to the foreign exchange subsystem. Now they pay me very well indeed, and I'm pretty sure that the guys in the foreign exchange department are glad to see me coming in the morning, but I'm a little surprised that a director would know my name."

"Jacques prides himself on keeping up," Burnham said.

"He must," Fredericks said.

Neither's smile changed as the drinks arrived.

With Fredericks's permission, Burnham ordered for them both, choosing the corned-beef hash which, he assured Fredericks, compared favorably with that of The University Club.

In his early sixties, Winthrop Burnham was lean, hollow-templed. His white hair was carefully barbered above his neat, small ears and he gave an impression of tautness that belied his years. His color, nonetheless, ran slightly more to *flambé* than to tan, and not even the exquisite suit could entirely mask the fact that his slimness derived more probably from a delicate digestion than from the habit of exercise.

Yet though physical force was no longer his, Burnham was clearly animated by another source of potency. His eyes, over the half-glasses, were clear and sharp, his fingers still and confident, and his firm voice familiar with the accents of command.

It was on the precise nature of this source of strength that Fredericks was speculating when he realized that he was being addressed.

"Before....?" Fredericks said.

"Before you began consulting privately," Burnham repeated, "or is that where one begins these days?"

Through the double-glazed window Fredericks

watched the small cars swarming soundlessly in the place below.

"I worked for the government," Fredericks said, "before."

"Yes?" Burnham, with bright interest, sat back.

"Yes," Fredericks said.

Across the sweep of the great place, above the Palais Bourbon, white clouds raced against the roiling blue.

"Another drink?" Burnham asked.

The corned-beef hash, though served on the sort of pewter salver more normally associated with *vol-au-vent* or calling cards, was, despite its imposing credentials, not sufficiently serious as cuisine to preclude the discussion of business.

"As you know, Mr. Fredericks," Burnham said, tearing a roll, "a significant portion of our business consists of representing American commercial interests in France."

Fredericks nodded, saying nothing, and Burnham noticed that he had not touched his food.

("He'll see you as a threat," they had said, "and one that he can't do anything about until he knows who sent you. Don't worry about his walking out. He wouldn't lose sight of you for the world.")

"We currently have a client," Burnham continued, helping himself to butter, "who is considering naming a newly elected Deputy to the National Assembly to the board of its French subsidiary. This subsidiary manufactures components for the SAR system of the NATO F-15 Strike Eagle...."

"SAR?"

"Sorry. Synthetic Aperture Radar. It's used for terrain masking and is considered very sensitive equipment. Now the vetting of such candidates is, normally, considered our responsibility. Given the fact, however, that the candidate is a sitting member of the host government, we would prefer not to involve ourselves directly."

("It doesn't make any difference *how* bald it sounds," they had said, "he'll already know that you're lying.")

"I'm not entirely sure how familiarity with French finance would help here, Mr. Burnham," Fredericks said pleasantly. "Surely you don't wish me to audit his books?"

"It's actually a bit more specific than that," Burnham said. "We've looked rather carefully, and for the life of us we can't figure out how he financed his campaign."

"We?" said Fredericks.

"Coffee?" Burnham asked.

"Please."

"Two," Burnham said to the waiter, who departed.

"Do I understand you correctly, Mr. Burnham," Fredericks asked, "to be saying that you'd like me to try to unbutton the campaign finances of a sitting French politician?"

"Unbutton," Burnham said brightly, "that's cryptographic jargon, isn't it?"

Fredericks smiled. "Two questions, if I may, Mr. Burnham."

"Certainly," said Burnham, patting his lips with his napkin.

"Who the hell are you? How did you know where to contact me?"

"I told you," Burnham said, "Jacques Rondet of Crédit Lyonnais volunteered...."

"No," said Fredericks, the voice still soft. "The

only number that they have for me is an answering service; the only address, a post office box."

"Ah," said Burnham brightly, astonished at the steadiness of his voice, "I suppose that it must have been another friend, then."

With a conscious effort of will, he forced himself to meet Fredericks's eyes. As he did so, he became acutely aware of his own smell, a sudden sharp tang of male acid, which he supposed to be an involuntary animal response to the presence of death.

"I understand, of course," Burnham said, "that this sort of thing is a bit out of your normal line. We feel, however, that the compensation that we're prepared to offer takes that fact generously into consideration."

"Go ahead," Fredericks said.

"Five hundred a day, U.S.," Burnham said, "all expenses, with thirty days guaranteed, up front."

"Fifteen thousand dollars," Fredericks said reflectively.

("A little carrot, a little stick," they had said, "we can use money and the broad. The important thing is that he get the feeling that you're going by the book, *particularly* if it doesn't feel like *our* book.")

"Exactly," Burnham said, "and the taxes are your business. Surely you and your lovely friend could put such a sum to good use."

Fredericks leaned across the table and put his hand on Burnham's arm.

"Which friend is that, Mr. Burnham?" he asked softly.

To his credit, Burnham actually managed to meet Fredericks's eyes as he responded.

"Why, the friend with whom you live in the Marais, Mr. Fredericks," he said. "The one who did the Hermès collection this afternoon at two. The one who's doing the Balmain collection next week. The one who rides a moped in Paris traffic. Every day."

"Ah," Fredericks said after a long moment, "*that* friend."

"And would cash or a check be better for you, Mr. Fredericks?" Burnham continued brightly. "Either is possible."

"Check," said Fredericks finally, "let's say a check."

His expression, as he withdrew his hand from Burnham's arm, was one of temporary regret rather than final disappointment, the expression of a man who has responsibly deferred a pleasure, not that of a man who has reconciled himself to its loss.

"Cassin," Burnham said. "C-a-s-s-i-n. First name Jean-Jacques. Elected last year to the National Assembly as an RPR deputy from the Yvelines. Midforties, lives outside Paris in le Pecq, married, three kids. Second son of a wealthy family from the Beauce, and squarely in the tradition of second sons has been running a negative cash flow since his thirties...."

"Let's get on with it, shall we?" Fredericks said.

"He mounted an impressive campaign last year," Burnham continued, "running very much on the family name but *not*, that's *not*, on the family money."

"For Christ's sake," Fredericks muttered.

"All right," said Burnham, coloring. "Six months ago, Jean-Jacques put together a syndicate to underwrite the purchase of a large parcel of land at Saint-Lô, in the Manche. The purchase was speculative, the mortgage taken back by the selling party against a minimal downpayment. The syndicate pays interest only for the first five years."

Fredericks shrugged.

"You should know," added Burnham, "that four of the six members of the syndicate are also deputies. They trust Monsieur Cassin, you see."

"So what?"

"As I believe I told you," sniffed Burnham in his lawyer's voice, "the nature of the equipment that our client manufactures is such that the appearance of security is very nearly as important as the security itself. A scandal of any sort is unthinkable. Monsieur Cassin's purchase is a speculative one, and is, thus, a potentially exposed position. We should simply like to be able to assure our client that it poses no potential embarrassment."

"Potentially exposed, potentially embarrassing," Fredericks's voice was suddenly sharp. "The way you've described it, the only exposure exists as a paper liability. The worst that could happen to Cassin and his friends would be to lose the little downpayment and some interest. What are you really worried about, Mr. Burnham?"

But Burnham, his briefcase in his lap, preferred not to hear the question.

("He *has* to know who you are, whom you represent," they had said. "If Cassin is the only hook you give him, he's got to go take a look at Cassin. No choice at all. And that, Mr. Burnham, is all you need.")

"The particulars, such as we know them,"

Burnham said, handing Fredericks a manilla envelope. "It's not much. We'd like more."

Fredericks's chair was already pushed back from the table when Burnham spoke again, carefully.

"There *is* one more thing, Mr. Fredericks." Occupied with his briefcase, Burnham did not look up as he spoke. "Jean-Jacques Cassin's elder brother, I believe, is himself a government functionary. It would be particularly unfortunate if he should become prematurely aware of our inquiries into Jean-Jacques's affairs."

("Just touch the brother lightly," they had said, "lightly and *badly,* Fredericks'll fill in the blanks *real* fast.")

"A government functionary," Fredericks repeated slowly.

"Exactly," said Burnham. "Some senior civil service sort, I believe. You'll be discreet, won't you?"

"Tell me, Mr. Burnham," Fredericks asked, "are you *worried* that Jean-Jacques Cassin has something embarrassing in his closet, or are you, rather, *hopeful* in that regard? It would be a help to know."

Burnham neither smiled nor responded as he called for the check.

Lunch concluded and details arranged, Burnham walked Fredericks to the street entrance of the Automobile Club. There he shook Fredericks's hand, wishing him good luck and goodby.

As Burnham watched Fredericks slip into the crowd and disappear, he became conscious of a slight feeling of chill, which he realized, recalling his hand in Fredericks's, to be fear.

Knowing what he knew of Fredericks from his

dossier, and knowing, as Fredericks did not, what was to come, Burnham permitted himself one brief and deeply felt prayer—that, as he had been assured, he would never see Noah Fredericks again.

As he signaled for a taxi, Winthrop Burnham looked casually around.

Although even his practiced eye could not see the photographers for whom he had walked Fredericks to the steps, he knew that they were there.

The battered DS Citröen turned from the place de la Concorde into the rue Royale, toward the Madeleine.

The driver lit a fresh *Disque Bleu* with the stub of its predecessor, flipping the butt from the window.

When the radio crackled, the man in the passenger seat finished detaching the telephoto lens from a 35mm camera before he responded with a laconic *"Oui?"*

"Ça va?" The voice was harsh with nicotine and electricity.

"Absolutely," the man said, in brutal, classless French, "front, side, and back. Fucker'll want enlargements for his mother, he ever sees these. Out."

There was a burst of static and then silence, as the car headed north, through the dying tag-end of the gray March day toward the grayer twentieth arrondissement and an anonymous block of buildings in the boulevard Mortier.

FIVE

THEY TOOK FREDERICKS in a gray van with heavy wire mesh on the windows and rear doors, leaving a sobbing Danielle behind with three policemen. Fredericks's arms were handcuffed behind him and fastened to an iron bar that ran the length of the bench on which he sat. The policeman to his right held the end of a chrome chain attached to leg manacles. Another policeman sat to his left. Fredericks was naked to the waist, and the angle of his arms had started the shoulder wound seeping again.

They crossed the Seine at the place de l'Hôtel de Ville. Through the mesh Fredericks could see couples chatting in the cafes bordering the place, and could smell the dank, fresh-water, potato odor of the river. The van in which they rode, to Fredericks a horror, attracted no more attention than if it had been a sports car. Outside, freedom was everywhere about them, as palpable as air and as unattainable as grace.

Once across the bridge, they turned immediately into the courtyard that housed the emergency service of the hospital Hôtel Dieu. There the policeman whom Fredericks had struck was helped out, cursing hoarsely and coughing blood. The dark-haired man in civilian clothes also left the van, returning in a few minutes with a clearly nervous young doctor carrying a medical bag.

Under the watchful eyes of four policemen, Fredericks's hands were detached from the bar behind him and refastened in front of him. Without speaking the young doctor took Fredericks's pulse and then examined the wounds in his forearm, shoulder, and back.

The doctor straightened and spoke to the man in the suit.

"Perhaps one or two stitches in the back," he said.

"Can you do it here?" the dark-haired man asked.

"Absolutely not!" the young doctor said indignantly, "In a filthy..."

"Then forget it," the dark-haired man shrugged. "Nothing serious, right?"

"Knife wounds are *always* serious," the young doctor said sternly. "There is the question of sepsis, of severe shock...."

"Sonny," the dark-haired man said easily, "your patient here's just killed one cop and almost torn the head off a second one. I don't think we'll worry too much about the shock. Now you just put on a Band-Aid or whatever it is you *can* do, and do it quick, okay?"

The dark-haired man said this clearly and slowly, and Fredericks had the sense that he was intended to overhear. His response, therefore, was obligatory.

"Cop?" Fredericks said. "There's been a mistake...."

"Yours, my friend," the dark-haired man said with satisfaction, "and you're in shit up to the neck."

"...*dans la crotte jusqu'au cou,*" was the way he put it.

Leaving the hospital, they recrossed the river to the Right Bank, turning behind the Hôtel de

Ville into the place Baudoyer. There the dark-haired man in civilian clothes, quite clearly in charge, descended from the van and entered the Commissariat Saint-Gervais, leaving Fredericks with four policemen in the van. The policemen did not speak while they waited, even among themselves, and regarded Fredericks, to his interest, with what seemed more curiosity than antipathy.

Once inside, Fredericks's in-take processing at the precinct house was brief. The dark-haired man had obviously taken care of the necessary paperwork, and he stood silently by as a nervous desk officer sounded the formalities.

"Name?" the officer asked.

"While walking home this evening," Fredericks said evenly, "I was attacked by three men in the rue des Blancs Manteaux. I managed to defend myself and return to my home. I was in the process of calling the police...."

"Save it," the dark-haired man said, in easy English.

"Nationality?" the desk officer asked.

"....when, following forcible entry, I was *again* attacked," Fredericks continued, "this time by the proud forces of the Police judiciare under the supervision of your natty friend there."

The dark-haired man smiled.

"Date of birth?" the desk officer asked.

"I demand that the American Consulate be notified of my detention," Fredericks said firmly. "I demand immediate legal representation and the services of a translator, and, if you would be so good as to lend me a *jeton*, I would like to exercise my constitutional right to make a phone call."

"What!?" the desk officer cried indignantly.

"Never mind," the dark-haired man said, then

turned to Fredericks and said, again in English, "About through?"

"Shit," Fredericks replied, also in English, "if the cops here ever saw one of those little plastic Miranda cards, they'd go nuts."

"The rights of the accused are not what they might be in France," the dark-haired man smiled.

"Good food, though," Fredericks said.

"I'm afraid that I won't be seeing you again, Mr. Fredericks," the dark-haired man said. "Good luck."

"You bet," Fredericks said.

The enforcement of the antiprostitution laws in Paris constitutes a rare example of Gallic efficiency. Each hooker is arrested about every two weeks at a scheduled time and place, held for twelve hours, fined, and released, thus providing the local commissariats with a nightly bag to bring up the numbers while interfering minimally with business.

In the early days of this arrangement, those whores whose night it was to go in the tank were often found assembled at the appointed corner, dressed in old clothes, carrying sleeping bags, bottled water, and garlic sausages, angrily rejecting untoward advances until the arrival of the paddy wagon.

This was keenly felt to be a violation of the spirit, if not the letter, of the agreement, and in subsequent renegotiation the police obtained a minimum standard of dress and *maquillage* for Bust Night in return for immediate visiting privileges, during which the old clothes, water, and sleeping bags could be delivered by the girls' colleagues.

Occasionally, of course, the amenities arrived

before the prisoners, but such merely logistical embarrassments aside, the arrangement has proven admirably functional.

The holding cell at the Commissariat Saint-Gervais that evening, made of heavy wire and filled with streetwalkers from the Porte Saint-Denis, looked like the girls' locker room at some particularly senior Senior Prom. Fancy dresses on hangers hung on the inside of the wire; whores in curlers dozed, chatted, and smoked.

Fredericks was handcuffed to a chair and watched by two policemen as the whores were rousted from the cage for transportation to the nearby Commissariat Saint-Paul.

It appeared that Fredericks was to have a private room. This courtesy worried him. If the man he had stabbed when he was attacked was, indeed, both a cop and dead, the press would not be far behind. For such a presentation, the police would need a cell that looked like a cell, not a powder room.

What happened next, therefore, while unpleasant, brought to his situation a welcome and very nearly compensating clarity.

Fredericks was locked into the wire cage with his arms still manacled behind him. In order for the handcuffs to be removed, he had to stand with his back to the locked door and put his wrists through the square hole that was in the door for that purpose.

When he did so, a fat sergeant who had been one of the arresting party slipped his baton through the handcuffs, twisted Fredericks's hands until the fingers were between the baton and the edge of the steel partition, and then, leaning his weight against the baton, crushed them.

Fredericks's little finger broke with the sound of a shingle snapping.

"A present from Jean-Luc, you bastard!" the sergeant snarled with rich satisfaction. "Remember it next time you feel like punching a cop."

Punch, not stab, thought Fredericks, quite clearly. The Algerian had not been a cop.

"Arnaud! No! You asshole!" Another policeman shoved the fat sergeant away from the door. "He belongs to *la piscine!* You piss off those bastards and you'll spend the rest of your goddamned service beating the bricks in Belleville!"

The French *Service de Documentation et de Contre-Espionage* (the acronym for which— SDECE—is pronounced suh-DECK) overlooks, from its offices in the boulevard Mortier, the public swimming pool in the Parc des Tourelles.

For this reason, the service is referred to in the *milieu* as "the swimming pool"—*la piscine*.

As the pain in his hand settled to a steady ache, Fredericks wondered briefly about Jean-Jacques Cassin and about his brother, the "senior civil service sort."

About Winthrop Burnham, Fredericks no longer wondered at all. He merely reflected to himself that it might be a rather long time before he regained his freedom, and he hoped that Burnham, given his age, would not die of natural causes first.

SIX

THE NIGHT WAS long in passing. The shirt that Fredericks had been given was too small, tight across the shoulders, pressing against the bandages. Fever made him thirsty.

It began to grow light outside around 4:30 A.M. Birds began singing around 5:00. At 8:00 the shift in the Commissariat changed. At 9:20 they came for him.

There were three men. Two wore suits, the third a jacket and slacks. They had pistols in shoulder holsters beneath their coats.

They presented papers to the desk officer, signed others. There was no unnecessary conversation.

The desk officer and the man in the jacket approached the door of the cage. The man in the jacket removed a pair of handcuffs from the back of his belt and motioned to Fredericks.

Fredericks smiled, shook his head, and held up his right hand. The little finger, bending away at an angle below the joint, was badly swollen, blue-black, save for a line of dark red that followed the edge of the broken bone.

"What happened?" the man in the jacket asked the desk officer.

"He fell down," the desk officer said.

"That what happened?" the man in the jacket asked Fredericks.

"Nope," Fredericks said. "It was broken by a fat sergeant on the four-to-twelve shift, first name Arnaud."

The man in the jacket turned and stared at the desk officer. "I want a full report. Typed and delivered by noon. I *don't* want it to say he fell down. I *do* want a last name for our friend Arnaud. You understand?"

"Hey, wait," the desk officer said, raising his hand, "I wasn't even..."

"Shut up," the man in the jacket said. "Don't talk. Just do it."

He turned back to Fredericks. "Listen, I have to put handcuffs on you. But we can do it in front, and I'll be careful, all right?"

Fredericks put his hands through the hole in the door and his wrists were fastened.

The three men led him from the commissariat into the sunlit square.

Outside, incredibly, it was simply a Tuesday morning.

Across the square was the playground of an elementary school. The children stopped playing to crowd against the fence, staring silently in horror and fascination at Fredericks, unshaven, shirt open across his thick flat chest, handcuffs bright in the morning sun.

As they were only six blocks from his street, Fredericks hoped very much that none of his soccer-playing friends were there.

"He eats little kids who don't do their homework," called the man in the jacket, *"raw!"*

The children's eyes widened, and they moved closer together.

Transportation this time was an unmarked station wagon. Fredericks sat in the back between two of the men. The third drove. They inched along in the heavy morning traffic on the rue de Rivoli, past the Louvre and the Palais Royal.

The car radio, tuned to France-Inter, offered popular music and testimonials to toilet tissue and detergents. Again, no one in the street paid the least attention to the car or its occupants.

When they reached the Tuileries, they turned right and moments later parked in the small place du Marché Saint-Honoré. On the radio, just before the car was turned off, a spokesman for Club Mediterranée reminded them that there was only one month of August.

Inside, a sign over the doors identified the building as the Troisième Brigade Territoriale and prohibited entry to all but authorized personnel.

On the third floor Fredericks was given a large brown envelope into which to put the contents of his pockets and his watch. Also his shoelaces and belt.

Here there were real cells, with bars. There were four in the block into which Fredericks was put. All were empty save his.

After an hour or so, a police medic accompanied by two uniformed guards came and, without comment, set, splinted, and taped Fredericks's finger.

In the early afternoon Fredericks was taken from the cell and led down a short hall to an office on the door of which was stenciled *"M. Bourrelier: Inspecteur Principal."*

Behind the desk sat a sweating, porcine middle-aged man in shirt sleeves and suspenders. His complexion was red, his graying hair brush-cut, and with his tie loosened against his fat chest he looked more like a cop than he would have in uniform.

Three crusher-types in equally plain clothes

lounged against the walls. Fredericks wondered briefly if he were to be softened for questioning, but, since he had not been handcuffed, guessed that the crushers were merely the fat inspector's security blanket.

The inspector let Fredericks stand in front of the desk for a few minutes as he read and shuffled papers. Once he said something that Fredericks could not catch, and the crushers laughed. In the small office Fredericks could smell him, stinking of sweat, red wine, and a sweet cologne.

Finally he looked up and leaned back, pig-eyed and arrogant. He sucked his teeth for a minute, spat a particle of food to one side, and then said, "Where's the knife?"

"What knife?" Fredericks asked.

"We looked for it," the inspector said. "Tore the fuckin' apartment apart. Closets, drawers, books, mattress, the works. We looked in the elbow joints of the drains and went through all the shit at the bottom of the airshaft. Nothing. So, where is it?"

"I don't know what you're talking about."

"We even strip-searched your broad, there," said the fat man. "Thought she might have it in her cunt or up her ass. *Nice* cunt, *nice* ass, but *no* knife. Least not that any of us could reach, and most of us tried."

The killing anger came like an old familiar illness. It was, as it had been before, less rage than decision, less emotion than the cold presence of the simple option, posed as a problem of logic: *I can't kill you now, therefore I'll kill you later*.

Though Fredericks neither moved nor spoke, such logic has a presence: the crushers no longer leaned but crouched, and Inspector Bourrelier in his chair brought his feet beneath him.

"C'mon," he said, tight-voiced, "try it." But Bourrelier was dead, and nothing that he might say or do mattered now to Fredericks.

Fifteen minutes later, Fredericks was offered a prepared statement to sign. When he did not read it, it was read to him. Forty-five minutes later, having neither signed the statement nor said another word, Fredericks was returned to his cell. There he sat throughout the afternoon and evening, empty of emotion and very nearly of thought, patiently waiting for the first team who, he knew, would come when they were ready.

Two Septembers past, Fredericks and Danielle had gone for the weekend to Villars, in the Alps.

They were newly together, their delight in each other radiant. Parents with children nodded to them with familiar, inclusive ease, and the normally fierce yard dogs of the mountain villages approached them wagging; intoxicated, Danielle had claimed, by their smell.

From the terrace of their hotel the valley of les Diablerets yawned away beneath them, dizzying, impossible, the abyss of dreams. There an old man had approached them, offering Danielle a pebble.

"Throw it," he had said smilingly to her, nodding at the air beyond the rail. "It will land, by foot, a week away."

Danielle, suddenly fearful, pinched and white, had declined and quickly excused herself, leaving Fredericks to reassure the embarrassed and apologetic old man, whose only wish had been to charm her.

Though Fredericks could not recall sleeping that night in his cell, he must have done so, however briefly, for once, quite clearly, he saw Danielle on

51

the same terrace, wearing the same lilac sun dress that she had worn in Villars.

She was bent backward over the wooden table, her dress above her waist, pinned there by faceless men.

And as Bourrelier, with dirty hands, parted her thighs, Fredericks, like the offered pebble, plunged and dwindled into an abyss without end, until he could no longer hear her cries, nor she his.

In the morning a diminutive functionary who identified himself grandly as "Hussier du Justice et Audiencier du Tribunal de Grande Instance de Paris" stood with a guard outside Fredericks's cell and, reading in a sing-song voice from a beribboned dossier, informed him that he stood accused of *"délits prévus par les articles* 1, 20, *et* 32 *du décret du* 18 *Avril* 1939 *modifié par l'ordonnance du* 10 *Julliet* 1958," and did he understand?

This time only the guard was required to sign.

In the afternoon he was again taken to the office of Inspector Bourrelier.

The interview was not a success.

Thus it was not until Wednesday night, at what Fredericks guessed to be about 11:00 P.M., that the next phase began.

SEVEN

ALTHOUGH THE MAN looked like the senior partner of a senior bank, Fredericks assumed that he was not.

And although the expressionless young adjutant who had ushered him into the clearly borrowed office on the second floor of the Troisième Brigade Territoriale marked *Circulation Routière*, addressed him as "Colonel," thus suggesting that he might be a military man, Fredericks again assumed that he was not.

Round, balding, dressed in ill-fitting and expensive clothes, the man made an incongruously avuncular impression. His eyes, behind round spectacles, were moist and large, and his voice, as he rose to greet Fredericks, seemed very nearly solicitous.

"Laloux," he said, offering his name as though in apology for the hour. "Won't you please sit down?"

Fredericks did so.

"Would you care for coffee, Mr. Fredericks?" he asked, moving a chair, with some difficulty, around to the far end of the desk, on which sat a flat tape recorder.

"Please," said Fredericks.

"Ask Jean-Claude to bring us coffee," Laloux said to his hard-faced young factotum at the door. "Also a bottle of Vittel and some aspirin."

The young man opened the door, spoke briefly, closed it.

Laloux regarded Fredericks thoughtfully for a moment before he spoke.

"Two things before we begin, Mr. Fredericks, may I?"

Fredericks nodded.

"First, there will have to be a formal record of our conversation. It can either be taken down verbatim by a stenographer, or it can be recorded and transcribed. It is my experience that the 'off' switch of the tape recorder will permit us a bit more latitude in our conversation than might otherwise be possible. Have you any objections?"

With a back-up recorder, a bit more latitude in editing and mix, too, Fredericks thought.

"That would be fine."

"Second," Laloux said, "I would ask you to keep clearly in mind the gravity of the offenses with which you are charged."

Fredericks noted the plural.

"If there are extenuating circumstances which would mitigate in your behalf, it is important that the *Juge d'Instruction* be made aware of them. It is, therefore, in your interest to be as forthcoming as possible. Do you understand?"

"Absolutely," Fredericks said.

"Excellent," said Laloux, smiling encouragement at Fredericks for his cooperation, "shall we begin, then?"

He depressed a switch on the tape recorder and, noiselessly, the reels began to turn.

Laloux opened a manilla folder on the desk. For a moment he read, turning pages. Then he spoke. "Fifteen April. Third Territorial Brigade. Present—Laloux, Martel. First interrogation of last name Fredericks, first name Noah. Band one, side one." He smiled at Fredericks. "Labels fall off."

"Cheap glue," Fredericks said.

"Mr. Fredericks, we are interested in determining two things. The first of these is who you are, and the second, what you are doing. We'll get to Monsieur Cassin, but first we'll begin with some background information, shall we?"

"Sure," Fredericks said, shaken, but determined for the moment not to show it.

"Your name is Noah Fredericks?"

"Yes."

"Born New York City, 21 April 1945, father Graham, mother Margaret, maiden name Hamilton, both deceased, no siblings?"

That could come from a residence card or work permit, thought Fredericks. "Yes."

"And you attended elementary and secondary schools in Greenwich, Connecticut?"

"You don't pronounce the 'c' in Connecticut," Fredericks said.

Laloux smiled, then reading from the dossier, chopped Fredericks off at the knees.

"Undergraduate degree in modern languages, Columbia University, 1966. Master's degree in history, also from Columbia University, 1968. The subject of your thesis was 'European Historiography of Soviet Foreign Policy: 1944–1952.' Is that right?"

Pain lanced up Fredericks's arm as he involuntarily clenched his hands.

"Mr. Fredericks?"

"Yes," Fredericks said. "That's right."

"And then?"

"I went to work," Fredericks said. "For IBM in New York. Trainee systems analyst."

57

"Odd choice for a historian," Laloux said.

"No choice at all," Fredericks said. "A boy has to eat."

"And how long were you there?"

"A year. A year and change."

"Seventeen months," Laloux said, not looking at the dossier. "Until November of 1971."

"That sounds about right," Fredericks said. "Go ahead."

"Then I got a job in Washington, D.C."

"Doing?"

"Data processing work. Systems analysis, file structure...."

"Data processing work?"

"Right."

"For whom?"

"The Department of State."

"Data processing work for the Department of State?"

Fredericks said nothing, waiting.

"Any special branch?" Laloux asked.

"The main branch, there, on Constitution Avenue."

Laloux permitted himself a smile.

"Mr. Fredericks," he said, "you were employed as a 'researcher,' whatever that might mean, at the National Foreign Assessment Center, were you not?"

"Ah," Fredericks said. "*I* see what you mean. Yes, that was it."

"Mr. Fredericks," Laloux said, "what is the Washington, D.C. area code?"

"Two-oh-two."

"And if you wanted to call, say, the CIA, in Langley, Virginia, what's *that* area code?"

"I have no idea."

"Well," Laloux said, "it's actually seven-oh-three, but you don't need to remember it. As long as you know the Washington area code and the number for the National Foreign Assessment Center, you can talk to the same people."

An utter weariness washed over Fredericks, sapping him as a chess player is sapped in the moment when the possibility of loss changes, if only subjectively, to certainty.

"Oh, Jesus," he said, with unfeigned fatigue, "in your business I suppose that seeing things under the bed is an occupational hazard, but just leave me the hell out, all right? Listen. I was a $22,000-a-year systems analyst, your basic electronic archivist. You've got a bunch of myopic clerks in visors cutting out clippings on every boring thing under the sun—Nigerian production of industrial diamonds, North Sea shipping rights, agricultural production figures for the province of Kosovo, you name it. It was my lofty responsibility to make sure that this useless shit was dutifully transcribed onto 600 BPI mag tape, and, further, to so structure and cross-reference the files that maybe it could be found again, anybody ever wanted to see it, which, of course, they didn't. That was it. Nothing more exciting than that.

Laloux smiled.

"Mr. Fredericks," he said, "let me tell you two stories, may I?"

"Certainly," Fredericks said.

"In the spring of 1972," Laloux began, "the American consulting firm of McKinsey & Co. received a contract for the on-site implementation of a computerized trading and financial system for the Yugoslav firm of SERPSI-EXPORT."

Like a crystal bowl shattering in slow motion, Fredericks's world disintegrated. For an appalling moment, he felt actual nausea, a physical dizziness, for there was only one possible source for the dossier from which Laloux was reading.

Laloux paused and regarded Fredericks, less for confirmation of those things he already knew than with the simple curiosity as to how a man's face might look in the moment when he realizes, without possible doubt, that he has been betrayed.

When Fredericks remained expressionless, Laloux affected a small *moue* of disappointment and continued.

"In June of that year," he said, "they dispatched a five-man team to Belgrade to work with SERPEX personnel on the implementation of the system. One of the McKinsey consultants was a young systems analyst named Frank Hamilton. Perhaps you know him?"

"No," Fredericks said.

"I suppose that there are many systems analysts in America." Laloux sighed.

"Like flies," Fredericks said.

"Now Mr. Hamilton was a new employee—as McKinsey was later, and uselessly, to point out—and, surprise, a speaker of Serbo-Croat. He did not, therefore, spend all of his time with the fellow members of his project team drinking beer in the upstairs bar of the Hotel Moskva and counting the days till parole, but rather took advantage of the opportunity to listen to the views of the Yugoslav Man In The Street. Well, there are a lot of men and a lot of streets, and at the end of three weeks Mr. Hamilton had the UBDA watchers folding at the knees...."

"UDBA?" Fredericks asked.

"I beg your pardon," Laloux said. "An acronym for the Yugoslav secret police.

"Ah," Fredericks said.

"Finally," Laloux continued, "they decide that he's just a sociable fellow, and they put him on a back burner, keep him company for a day every two weeks or so, but that's it. Therefore, when Mr. Hamilton makes a reservation for two at the Hotel Varadin in Novi Sad—and leaves with some Italian girl he has picked up in Skadarlija—the watchers figure that it's just a dirty weekend on the Danube and let him go without a sitter."

For the first time, it occurred quite clearly to Fredericks that Laloux had not so much as mentioned the Algerian he had stabbed, nor asked a single question about Jean-Jacques Cassin.

"Which is a mistake," Laloux continued, "for in Novi Sad Hamilton meets with some other men in another street, who are *not* exactly Men In The Street; specifically, a TANYUG correspondent, an associate editor of the dissident journal *Nasa Réc*, and two dissident academics—historians, I believe—who constitute the leadership of a group concerned with certain problems that they fear might arise in the years following the succession. Such as an excess of aid on the part of their large, northern neighbor in restoring 'stability' to the government of an historical ally, *à la* Budapest or Prague...."

"*A la* lots of places that used to be real, live countries," Fredericks said. "In their place I'd be worried, too."

"Now these people realize," Laloux continued, with an inexorability that ignored, oddly, whatever Fredericks might have to say, "that unilateral military resistance in the face of such an eventuality is not a feasible option. They suggest, however, that with a minimum of Western aid, a limited and short-term *maquis*-style resistance might be offered, which could provide enough photographs and command enough newspaper space to, at least, debunk the lie of 'invitation,' and, at most, legitimatize a government in exile. To this end, they have a rather precise shopping list, which they present to the versatile Mr. Hamilton, our quondam systems analyst. A list that includes such typical data processing equipment as infantry-form TOW missiles...."

"Look," Fredericks said, "I don't know what you're talking about."

"I'm sorry," Laloux said solicitously, "TOW is an acronym for a *T*ube-launched, *O*ptically-tracked, *W*ire-guided missile, a hand-held, anti-tank weapons system manufactured by Hughes International, perfectly proper both for town and country use...."

"No, no," Fredericks said. "I mean, why are you telling me this?"

"Bear with me, Mr. Fredericks," Laloux said softly, "this story is almost over."

But Fredericks already knew that.

"Mr. Hamilton, of course, realizes that these good people are out of their minds," Laloux continued, "and that the probability of the United States government smuggling arms to Yugoslav civilians is precisely zero. Still, the value of one more network in the Balkans, given the life expectancy of such networks, is not to be totally ignored. Mr. Hamilton, therefore, establishes some basic ground rules for communication, such standard EDP tradecraft as the establishment of cutouts, the setting up of dead drops, and the priming of safe houses, and leaves, fast."

"Is that it?" Fredericks asked wearily.

"Well," Laloux said, "almost. You see, it turned out that the TANYUG correspondent, one Veljko Maričić—was getting two paychecks in those days, and the second one was from UDBA."

The names came like deliberate blows.

"Lazar Todorović. Branko Simać. Matija Keković and his wife. UDBA had them for almost two weeks, I hear, before they were shot. Twelve others were imprisoned. Mr. Hamilton was called to the United States on urgent personal business. So urgent, indeed, that the secret police who went to the Hotel Moskva hoping that he might help them with their inquiries found his clothes still in the room. *You* know how it is when you're in a rush; barely time to wipe the room for prints before you have to run."

"What do you want?" Fredericks asked helplessly.

"I'm just curious, Mr. Fredericks," Laloux said. "Have you never heard this story before? I mean, it didn't make the papers, but it caused quite a bit of noise at the time, and Washington is a small town when it comes to gossip."

"No," Fredericks said, "I hadn't heard it."

"Well," Laloux sighed, "perhaps you've heard the second story."

"Not if it's like the first, I haven't."

"Let's try anyway, shall we?" Laloux's pale, hunter's eyes were on Fredericks. "We'll call this story, let's see, how about 'The Tale of Two Conventions'?"

He spoke with bright good humor, as though proposing a party game, and again Fredericks was aware that his responses, even his presence, seemed oddly irrelevant to the proceedings, that he had been asked no question to which the answer was not already known. Indeed, the process seemed more one of expository soliloquy than of interrogation.

"What the hell do you want?" Fredericks asked.

"This story takes place right here in Paris, sixteen months after the first story, in October of 1973. From the twelfth to the nineteenth of that month there took place the OECD Congress on Trade with the Non-aligned Nations. This was, of course, covered by most of the major wire services, and the TANYUG correspondent was our old friend, Mr. Veljko Maričić, remember him?"

"Sure, the bad guy from the first story."

"That would depend on your point of view, I suppose," Laloux said.

"I'm an American," Fredericks said. "That *is* my point of view."

"Yes," Laloux said, "yes, I suppose it might be. It was *not*, however, the point of view of the Yugoslav government when he was found."

"Found?"

"Yes," Laloux said. "Comrade Maričić was staying in the Hôtel Tremoille, or at least he *should* have stayed in the Tremoille, nice and bright around the Tremoille, plenty of cops.

"Instead, he apparently got a little drunk one evening and decided to go whoring in the rue Quincampoix. You know that quarter?"

"Sure," Fredericks said. "Over near Rambuteau."

"Exactly," Laloux said. "A bad idea. Lots of dark little corners there and not so many cops. And somewhere between one and four in the morning, on the night of 16 October, something nasty came out of the dark and got him."

"Mugger?" Fredericks knew that if he stopped speaking he would not speak again.

"Something a bit meaner than your average mugger, if you listen to the coroner's office," Laloux said. "He got broken up like a wooden doll, in a dark little *ruelle* not eight feet from the sidewalk. People *had* to be passing the alley mouth while he was being taken apart. But nobody heard anything, nobody saw anything."

"A better story," Fredericks said.

"It is," Laloux agreed. "But not for the reason you think. Now the second convention—remember?—took place the same week in Brussels." Laloux referred to the dossier. "NATO Conference on EDP Cartography Standards, it was. That's your field, is it not?"

"Except for the 'NATO' and the 'Cartography'," Fredericks said, no longer even trying, except for the form.

"Mr. Fredericks," Laloux said, "it is a convention in intelligence work that case officers do not reside, if possible, in the country that hosts their agents, but in its immediate neighbor. A case officer running a network in France, for instance, will, for reasons of legal convenience, most likely be resident in West Germany, say, or Belgium.

"For that reason, we maintain a close liaison with our sister services in the Benelux countries. Specifically, we share the names and photographs on our respective B-lists," Laloux explained.

"B-list?" Fredericks said.

"Possibles," Laloux said, "which is why this is a better story than the first one. You see," he smiled a bit awkwardly, "it's illustrated."

Laloux read from the file card attached to an 8 x 10 print. "October 10, 1973. NATO Conference on EDP Cartography Standards. Name: Pillsbury, John. Accreditation: U.S. Dep't. of State/NFAC."

Fredericks began to hum.

"Now the Yugoslavs, Mr. Fredericks, were utterly convinced that Maricić had been killed by the Americans because of his involvement in the Hamilton affair. Indeed, so convinced that they consented to provide us with a photograph they had taken of Mr. Hamilton. We, frankly, discounted their accusations. Imagine, then, our surprise when one of our file clerks—an archivist, like yourself—noticed that the 'Pillsbury' photograph and the 'Hamilton' photograph were of the same man. Enough to make your blood run cold."

Laloux paused.

"Would you like to *see* the photographs, Mr. Fredericks?"

Fredericks's humming was louder now, a bit more insistent.

"Mr. Fredericks?"

"No," Fredericks said, "no, thanks."

Despite the coolness of the rainy, night air blowing through the window gratings, the shirt that Fredericks had been given was soaked with sweat. Beneath the cheap fabric the clenched muscles of his back stood out in slabs.

Though Fredericks's thin stab wounds had closed, the raised bruises surrounding the punctures, which would endure for months as hard lumps just beneath the skin, were easily discernible.

Laloux pressed a switch on the tape recorder. The reels stopped abruptly, spilling them into silence.

"Phillipe." Laloux cleared his throat. "Would you get Jean-Claude, please, and return Mr. Fredericks upstairs. It's really much too late."

Laloux's young assistant opened the door and spoke to a shape standing in the darkened hallway.

"I'm sorry," Laloux said softly to Fredericks. "It was necessary." Glancing down, Laloux noticed Fredericks's broken finger, arched and white, the tip pressed hard against the splint, for pain.

"Tomorrow," he said gently, "tomorrow we will speak of Jean-Jacques Cassin."

Fredericks rose and turned toward the door.

"It will be all right," Laloux whispered, and it was difficult to tell whether he was addressing Fredericks or himself.

EIGHT

"So," LALOUX SAID the next afternoon, "perhaps you will tell us about your interest in Monsieur Jean-Jacques Cassin?"

"The interest isn't mine," Fredericks said, still logy from twelve hours of desperate, dreamless sleep.

Laloux waited patiently.

"On the twenty-fifth of March," Fredericks said, "I was retained by the firm of Jobert Frères to inquire into the details of a property syndication put together by Monsieur Cassin, as part of an investigation to determine..."

"With whom did you speak at Jobert Frères?" Laloux interrupted.

"Burnham," Fredericks said. "A Mr. Winthrop Burnham."

"Phillipe," Laloux said, scribbling something on a piece of paper, "would you please?"

The young man took the piece of paper, read it, and left the room.

"Please," Laloux said, "continue. Tell me what you did, and what you found out."

"I went to Saint-Lô," Fredericks said.

The reels began to turn again.

"The Préfecture of the Department of the Manche is *in* Saint-Lô," continued Fredericks. "Through Jobert Frères, I arranged a meeting with the Prefect. At this meeting, I explained to *Monsieur la Préfet* that I represented an American firm, nameless, of course, engaged in the sale of cosmetics in Europe on the home-party distribution system, interested in constructing a factory in the North, and attracted by the terms offered by the *zone industrielle* of Saint-Lô. Ding-dong, Avon calling, with 450 jobs, in other words."

Laloux smiled.

"He didn't get it," Fredericks said. "Deaf as a post, he was, also a little anti-American to boot. Kept on trying to tell me the history of Saint-Lô, showed me these pictures of the town taken in August 1944, just after the place had been bombed to rubble. By the Americans."

"Overliberated," Laloux said.

"Whatever," Fredericks said. "His Assistant for Departmental Development, however—one Roger Hanon—caught *right* on, and got very excited. Even told me his wife used to be personnel supervisor at the cheese processing plant, just in case we needed a local to flog the other locals, I guess."

Laloux, knowing that Fredericks had nothing left to hide, did not interrupt now.

"So this assistant," Fredericks continued, "bundles me into his Citröen and takes me on the grand tour.

"Now the property held by the Cassin syndicate lies north of the town, to the west of the N174, running from the city line to the Vire river. When we finally get there—and it took forever—I, of course, get all excited. We stop the car, I get out, pace off some distances, take down some lot numbers, play with a slide rule, the whole bit. And, actually, the land is pretty good. Two kilometers from the railhead, twenty-five from the N13, a river to handle the effluent, and three postal pickups a day, guaranteed. Time to go back to Hanon's office, do the maps and papers.

"Politicians, land, and a *zone industrielle.*" Fredericks counted on his fingers. "First you zone the land for sheep grazing, or the Maréchal Pétain National Park, whatever. Then, you buy it. Then you rezone it for factories and move to Antibes."

"That what happened?" Laloux asked.

"No," Fredericks said. "Surprised me, too. But the syndicate's land was already in the *zone industrielle,* had been for two years. Of course, its assessed value is nowhere near its resale value, but, basically, so far, so clean.

"The Deeds Registry is not much help. Land deals can be executed in the name of a lawyer, like stock held in a street name, and the syndicate's package is in the name of one Pierre Bichet, a local lawyer. I do, however, notice that the previous owner—and, presumably, the mortgage holder—is a Monsieur Jean-Serge Meillant who, Hanon informs me, is a very successful farmer with a place out on the Périers road and a bigwig in the local RPR. Cassin, you will recall, is an RPR Deputy. Not much, but something, so I arrange an appointment for the next morning with the lawyer, Bichet..."

"You spent the night in Saint-Lô?" Laloux asked.

"Hotel Crémaillère, on the place Préfecture," Fredericks snapped. "Night of April 7."

"Thank you," Laloux said. "Please go on."

Fredericks glared for a moment, white with anger, then continued.

"Maître Bichet turns out to be a fat old gravy-on-the-tie and straw-in-the-cuffs country lawyer, and he is not stupid at *all.* 'Ah, the Americans,' he says, when Hanon drops me off, like he was expecting me."

Laloux was suddenly very alert.

"We fence for a while," continued Fredericks. "I explain that my brief requires me to deal directly with the principals. He assures me that he speaks for the principal, and that I may deal in confidence with him. I assure him that I have no interest in doing so unless he *is* the goddamned principal."

"He used the singular, did he?" Laloux asked. "Principal?"

Fredericks's eyes lifted slowly and held Laloux in a cold gaze.

"Yes," he said. "He used the singular."

"Go ahead."

"Well, we go around a few times, but Bichet is not only not stupid, he is also not a virgin, and he doesn't need to be told you love him for himself before you can ask him to bend over. I don't think I'd been there thirty minutes before he was flirting with both feet in the air."

"Yes?"

"I was asking all about mortgages, liens, tax liability, God knows what, when he gets this woeful expression on his face. 'This used to be much simpler,' he said. 'Today, it's all so complex.' And he pulls this fat dossier out of his desk. 'Look at this,' he tells me, 'all of this paperwork just for the one parcel of land.' I'm not sure, but I think he actually fluttered his eyes.

"So we do a deal. I pay for the coffee if he goes and gets it. Five hundred U.S. a cup, and it'll take him a half-hour."

"Was it worth it?" Laloux asked, almost casually.

"Cost me a grand, I got paid fifteen, sure, it was worth it."

"The fat with the lean here, please," Laloux said.

"A very nice little deal," Fredericks said. "Cassin goes to his friends—fellow deputies, right? who have better things to do than run out to the Calvados and chat up some old farmer—and tells them, 'Hey, listen, I've got this sweetheart land deal.' And he explains to them how it works. There are two contiguous parcels of land, totaling roughly a thousand acres. He can get the package, he tells them, for a thousand dollars an acre—2 percent down, the rest in 7½ percent notes, interest only for the first five years, then the principal amortized over another ten. If they can sell the land at a profit in the first five years, they make a lot of money. If not, they just walk away, and all they lose is the 2 percent and a little interest. Now that is *admirable* leverage, and, of course, his buddies jump all over it...."

"I'm not sure that I understand," Laloux said.

"What's the problem?" Fredericks asked. "Dollars? Acres? A man in your position's gotta understand the world's reserve currency, Colonel."

"I'm not sure I see anything illegal."

"Ah," said Fredericks. "Then when I get to that part I'll go real slow, all right? Fraud for the Under-Fives, promise."

"Go ahead."

"The syndicate," Fredericks continued, "signs two notes for the land, which is not at all unusual. One for $800,000 to Meillant, another for $200,000, in trust for the Paris law firm of Cabinet Lalande. Now, got your pencil? Here comes the fraud part."

Laloux was listening carefully.

"Our friend Cassin, you see," Fredericks said, "didn't pay a thousand an acre. He bought both parcels from Meillant at eight hundred dollars the acre. The syndicate's $800,000 note takes care of that. The note to Cabinet Lalande is a $200,000 present to Cassin from himself, just because he's a nice guy and should have more money than he does. He even rides free on the syndicate's interest payments. Hell, the land's good. His friends'll probably make a little money and never even know that they got screwed."

"I see," Laloux said after a moment of silence.

"Sure," said Fredericks, "all he needed was a little trust."

"Not really the sort of thing that would help a man's political career," Laloux observed.

"Can't think how," Fredericks said.

"Mr. Fredericks," Laloux asked reflectively, "why do you think your employers wished such information?"

"Got me. Ask them."

"Actually," Laloux said, "we're doing that right now. I'd be interested, though, in your guess."

"They said they wished to establish Cassin's financial probity prior to his nomination to a corporate board," Fredericks said stiffly.

It sounded utterly ridiculous.

"And did you believe that?" Laloux asked politely.

"I don't know," Fredericks said, his face pallid with fatigue and shiny with sweat, "Cassin's an RPR Deputy, and there's no shortage of people who'd like to stick a finger in Chirac's eye."

"But that doesn't make sense, does it?" Laloux persisted. "I mean, Cassin's just a freshman deputy, his most important seat is on the Produce

76

Transport Committee. He's just not important enough to discredit a party, neither as an individual, nor as a symbol."

There was a knock on the door. Phillipe entered, gave Laloux a single piece of paper, and resumed his seat near the door.

Laloux read the paper carefully, put it to one side, and slowly addressed Fredericks.

"I'm afraid the people at Jobert Frères know nothing at all about Monsieur Cassin, Mr. Fredericks."

Outside an ambulance passed by, its strident high-low urgency welling suddenly, then receding.

"Mr. Fredericks?"

Fredericks had been betrayed; a man was dead at his hands, the woman he cared for violated, his freedom had been taken, and even the shirt on his back was not his own. Yet still he sat, silent, clenched in opposition.

"Inspecteur Bourrelier feels that your friend knows more than she has said," added Laloux, who understood that Fredericks needed help. "It wouldn't be fair to her to allow him to act on that supposition if it weren't true."

Fredericks's face, when finally he spoke, was bewildered, ashamed, his voice stiff.

"You stupid bastards," he said, "why can't you do your own homework? Cassin has a brother, an important brother. Maybe at the Elysées, maybe at the Quai d'Orsay, maybe DST or SDECE. Shouldn't take too long to find out. It's the brother they want. Their only interest in Jean-Jacques Cassin is in his usefulness as a means to compromise that brother...."

"I see," Laloux said, sitting back as the tension

seemed to drain from him. "Perhaps we should talk a bit about that?"

Laloux's voice was diffident, his manner in victory gracious.

At 6:00 that evening the interrogation ended.

Fredericks was given a paper sack from Prisunic containing a new shirt, a new belt, and new shoelaces.

Handcuffed unobtrusively to Phillipe and accompanied by Laloux and two other men in suits, he was led downstairs and outside to a waiting Renault 16 TS.

There were no uniformed police to be seen.

They were already into the thick evening traffic on the rue Saint-Honoré before Laloux spoke.

"Mr. Fredericks," he said, "you have been transferred into our custody for special interrogation. At 2:30 tomorrow afternoon, it will be reported to the Gendarmerie Nationale and to Interpol that you have escaped from that custody."

The car turned right on the rue Marengo. Fredericks wondered if they were going to kill him.

"Their search will be both genuine and energetic, and if you are apprehended there is nothing further we can do for you."

The car crossed the rue de Rivoli and entered the grounds of the Louvre.

Laloux handed Fredericks an envelope.

"Two hundred francs, Mr. Fredericks, and a ticket on Pan Am Flight 302, departing Orly for New York tomorrow at 2:00 P.M."

The Renault stopped in the car park nearest the Arc du Carrousel. Nearby, large tourist buses were slowly loading. In the gardens beyond, couples strolled slowly in the deepening evening light.

"Phillipe," Laloux said, and the handcuff was removed from Fredericks's wrist. The man to his right opened the door and got out, holding it.

"Don't come back to France, Mr. Fredericks," Laloux said. "Not ever."

Twenty feet from the car Fredericks stopped and turned, as though something had been forgotten, a question left unanswered. The car pulled slowly away from the curb.

A giant Mercedes bus, filled with tourists and bearing the legend "Paris by Night," passed slowly between them on balloon tires, roiling the air with diesel heat.

When it had passed, Fredericks was gone, leaving only the lovers, pigeons, the darkening shadows beneath the chestnut trees, and the oceanic sky, its blue the color of storms.

NINE

A LIBERTY THAT has been summarily suspended—and, as arbitrarily, restored—becomes a damaged quantity, stained and qualified. Yet in the gardens' thickening shadows, Fredericks felt very nearly drunk with freedom. The feeling was a sensual one, the soft intoxication of food, of wine, of sex. For a luxurious moment he embraced it as a sleeper, in the moment of waking, clings to a sweet dream.

It was the dinner hour, and the gardens were emptying. An *au pair* with an infant in a stroller passed, trailed by a small boy carrying a large and once-white plastic replica of the Concorde.

Regarding Fredericks's wink, quite properly, as an invitation, the little boy trundled over to the bench where Fredericks sat and announced with proprietary pride, *"J'ai un avion, moi!"* presenting the airplane for inspection.

"Mais il est trés, trés beau," Fredericks said after grave appraisal. *"Comment s'appelle-t-il, ton avion?"*

The boy stood first on one foot, then on the other, considering. Finally, standing on Fredericks's shoe and balancing himself with one hand on Fredericks's knee, he firmly piped, *"Il s'appelle Pierre."*

It seemed a particularly fine name for an airplane.

Fredericks watched the *au pair* and the children until they faded from sight beneath the shadows of the trees, leaving him with only ghosts for company, and the leaves that stumble, scraping, before the shepherd wind.

Fredericks crossed the river at the Pont des Arts. Beneath him the heavy evening traffic flowed in a liquid stream of moving lights. Fredericks could smell the sharp fumes from the cars and the dank, sweet, fresh-water smell of the Seine.

Reaching the rue Mazarine, he paused at a corner kiosk to purchase the newspapers. These he took with him as he entered a large *cafe-tabac* in the center of the block. The *tabac* was brightly lit and crowded. It was a popular café, serving the neighborhood horse players as the local PMU center, and serving Fredericks, for the extortionate sum of fifty francs a month, as a *poste-restante,* to which address each month for the past three years, as a matter of operational habit, Fredericks had sent himself assorted junk mail and a carefully sealed envelope containing five thousand dollars in Swiss hundred-franc notes, which he collected and remailed at the end of each month.

"Monsieur Pillsbury!" The proprietor bustled up, all smiles. *"Vous allez bien?"*

"Bien, merci," Fredericks said, putting a fifty-franc note on the glass. "Have I any mail?"

"Comme toujours," the proprietor said, bending and rummaging beneath the counter.

He placed Fredericks's packet of letters on the counter. The envelope was there.

"Chanteclair in Saturday's fifth at Auteuil," the proprietor said. "She is a certainty."

"Of course," Fredericks said, "and Bruges is the Venice of the North."

The proprietor cackled as the fifty-franc note disappeared beneath his hand.

Seated at a table in the rear, Fredericks asked for a *demi* and a *jambon-beurre*. The beer was cold and delicious. The sandwich, made on warm, fresh bread, was crusty and wonderful to smell. As he ate, Fredericks scanned the newspapers carefully.

Nothing.

When he had finished eating, he settled his bill and obtained a *jeton* for the telephone.

The phone was downstairs in the Tabac, next to the washrooms.

Danielle answered on the third ring.

Fredericks said, "It's me."

"Noah?" Her voice was leaden, distant. "Where are you?"

"I'm in the *quartier Latin*," Fredericks said. "I'll get a taxi, be there in fifteen minutes."

"I didn't know where you were." Danielle began to weep.

"It's all right, Dany," Fredericks said.

"No, it's not," Danielle said. "It's not all right at all."

"Fifteen minutes," Fredericks said, and hung up.

Outside, the weekend was beginning in the Latin quarter. There was a palpable air of gaiety, of pleasures imminent. The sidewalks were thronged with young people, the cafés bright with noise and zinc and language.

As the cab moved slowly through the thick traffic, Fredericks read the shop signs and the theater marquees.

Librarie, read one. *Papeterie*, read another.

Croque-Monsieur. Hot-Dog. And, on a cinema marquee: *La Nuit des Morts Vivants.*

Fredericks had the cab drop him at the mouth of their small street. The Sabbath had thinned the usual crowds, and by the time he reached the door of Danielle's building he had already made one pair of watchers, seated in an old black Citröen DS parked near the rue des Écouffes.

He did not care.

As he entered the door, it seemed inconceivable that only four days had passed since he had done so last.

"Noah?" Danielle said in a tremulous voice. Her eyes were swollen from weeping and her face lumpy with fatigue, or fear.

"I'm so sorry," Fredericks said. As he reached for her, her hands stopped his arms, holding him away.

"No, don't," she said. "I can't."

The apartment behind her had been neatened, but it was not the same as it had been. The plastic dust-cover of the stereo was gone, and the shelf above it which had held her glass animals was now bare. The hems of the curtains had been torn out, and his books were no longer in the bookshelves, but rather stood in stacks against the wall beneath, as though preparing for a trip.

Danielle turned from him and walked to the center of the room, hugging herself as if she were chilled. She did not look at him as she spoke.

"On Monday," she said, "I watched you hit a policeman. They told me that you'd killed another." Her voice began to shake. "So how can you be here now?"

Fredericks did not respond.

"The reason that I ask," she continued, her voice rising as it tried to outrace tears, "is that I don't *know!*"

Danielle was now weeping openly.

"What else don't I know, Noah? Do I know your real name? Do you have a wife? A child? Did you kill a man on Monday? You see, I don't *know* anything. They didn't believe me. You never told me anything, so I couldn't tell them anything, and they wouldn't stop.... No! Don't touch me!"

And as Danielle rocked and sobbed, Fredericks's soul recoiled upon itself—clenched and coiled around a center of hatred, and he was tense and black and unseeing. When her weeping was spent and she spoke again, her voice startled him, for there were no voices where he had been, but only night and fog and Bourrelier's death.

"There's whiskey if you want one," Danielle said.

"I have to go away," Fredericks said.

"When?" Danielle asked dully.

"Soon."

"Are they making you leave?"

"No," Fredericks said.

"Then why?" Danielle asked, her voice beginning to crack again. "Are you a criminal?"

"No."

"For God's sake," Danielle cried, "say something! Noah! Just one true thing! Anything...."

She wept.

"A long time ago," Fredericks began, "I was a young man, and in the exercise of that dispensation granted to the young, I held beliefs. I believed that Law and laws were different, and Law the elder. I believed that the responsibility for lives entrusted to one's care did not terminate upon the mere extinction of those lives. I believed in loyalty to one's allies and in the duty of resistance to tyranny....Ah," Fredericks bared his teeth in what he intended as a smile, "Lord Baden-Powell himself would have been embarrassed. I was very young, then."

"They said you were a *tueur à gages*," whispered Danielle, "a paid assassin!"

"Well," Fredericks said, "you know how people talk when they get excited."

"You're not coming back, are you?" Danielle said.

"I don't know," Fredericks said.

"Where are you going? What are you going to do? *Tell me!*"

"Like my new shirt?" Fredericks asked, holding the fabric toward her in his fingers.

"Noah!"

Fredericks's hand tightened slowly on the front of the shirt. The material stretched, then shredded with a harsh tearing sound across his back.

"Me neither," Fredericks said, the torn shirt dangling from his fist.

And then Danielle was tight against his bare chest, clinging desperately and sobbing, her face pressed deep into the hollow of his shoulder as he lifted her like a child and carried her to the bedroom above.

They made love with violent urgency, in that hunger born only of loss.

In passion she called his name.

And when she first woke, in the half-light of dawn with the sweet musk of their love still heavy in the air, he was gone.

TEN

It WAS BARELY light when Fredericks stepped into the street outside Danielle's building. He was wearing an expensive suit. A trench coat was draped over his right forearm and he carried a large suitcase in his left hand.

It was too early for taxis at the small queue nearby, so Fredericks began walking toward the place de l'Hôtel de Ville.

He walked with the light traffic down the rue Vielle du Temple. The only vehicles that came out of the small street behind him were a blue camionette marked "Malouf Plombiers" and a gray Peugeot sedan.

Fredericks turned right into the narrow rue Saint-Croix de la Bretonnierie, walking now against the traffic. When he reached the rue des Archives, he turned left toward the place de l'Hôtel de Ville. A moment later, reflected in a shop window, the gray Peugeot sedan appeared, idling along quietly behind a refuse truck.

At the second open café that he passed, the angle of the mirrors in the first being wrong, Fredericks entered and, standing at the bar, ordered a coffee and a small cognac.

After three coffees, and 45 minutes of very careful noting of those pedestrians who passed the café twice, Fredericks gave the barman ten francs and asked him to order a taxi. When the barman pointed out that there was a *Station de Taxi* not 50 meters from the café, Fredericks merely smiled stupidly and repeated his request, not bothering, under the circumstances, to explain that in the matter of baby-sitters a 50-yard headstart tends admirably to thin out the field.

Though moving with no apparent haste, Fredericks was out the door of the café and into the cab before it had blown its horn. In the light early-morning traffic as they drove quickly along the *quais* of the Left Bank toward the Aérogare des Invalides, Fredericks could see, in the driver's wing mirror, the gray Peugeot sedan following calmly behind them.

And with equal calm, as he watched the watchers, Fredericks reflected that now there were only the two in the car.

The sun had barely risen, striking shadows from the lamps on the Pont Alexandre III and turning the glass of the Petit Palais to mirror, when they arrived at the Invalides. Though Fredericks was certain that there had not been sufficient time to set up a front-tail, he was acting now from operational habit, and as he emerged from the cab and fumbled in his pocket for change he casually inspected the pedestrian traffic, looking for the classic two-three split favored by streetwatchers.

Nothing.

Fredericks paid the driver and entered the terminal.

Idling at the rear of the taxi queue, the two men in the Peugeot sedan watched Fredericks disappear inside. The driver, who was the elder of the two, said in a crude, military tone, "You stay with him. If he takes a bus, you walk with it out to the end of the ramp and I'll pick you up there. If it looks like he's goin' for a walk or anything, you give me a squawk on the box. I'll get us another car."

Without replying, the man in the passenger seat, a dark-haired, corpulent fellow, reached into the back seat of the Peugeot and picked up a cheap, plastic, salesman's sample case and a copy of *Le Figaro*. As he left the car and walked toward the terminal, he looked very much like the businessman or minor bureaucrat that he was not. Because of the hour, the lower level of the aerogare, from which the buses depart, was peopled only by a few early-rising businessmen, saving the taxi fare to Orly-Sud for connection with their internal Air-Inter flights. It therefore took the SDECE man following Fredericks only a few seconds to register that Fredericks was nowhere to be seen and, almost as quickly, to see Fredericks's suitcase and overcoat against the wall outside the men's room door. The SDECE man was a professional, for whom locating Fredericks's suitcase was clearly an inadequate substitute for locating Fredericks himself. Carrying the sample case and the folded newspaper in one hand and fumbling absently with his trouser buttons with the other, he crossed to the men's room, shouldered the door open, and passed inside.

It took seven minutes for the reinforcing pavement team and a second car to arrive, an operational lapse later bitterly criticized.

From that point on, however, the SDECE team moved with commendable speed.

Indeed, in less than three minutes they had located Fredericks's suitcase, subsequent examination revealing its contents to be wadded old clothes and a portable typewriter—the typewriter, it was generally and retrospectively agreed, for ballast.

And in less than five minutes they had found the SDECE man who had followed Fredericks into the terminal.

It was the driver who recognized his partner's shoes beneath the door of the toilet stall.

The sample case was beside him on the floor; the newspaper, neatly folded, lay on top. His trousers and underclothes had been carefully lowered to his ankles. Indeed, the only evidence to suggest that the man had not merely dozed off while relieving himself was a shattered wooden splint found behind the toilet and the responding physician's determination that, while the man would survive, both his skull and his collarbone had been fractured.

Fredericks emerged from the Métro at the station Richelieu-Drouot in the ninth arrondissement. The streets and sidewalks were filled with the morning shopping crowds. Fredericks walked north on the rue Laffitte, passing the Eglise Notre Dame de Lorette and entering the *quartier* of cheap cafés and porno cinemas south of Pigalle.

At a filthy café in the rue de Navarin that reeked of stale urine and coarse cigarettes Fredericks purchased a cognac and a *jeton* for the telephone.

The call was brief; the rendezvous arranged for 4:30 that afternoon.

When he had finished the cognac, he walked two blocks before finding a sex cinema in the rue Monnier whose marquee advertised *"L'Eté d'une teenager Suedoise! 24 Heures sur 24!"*

The cinema was pitch dark, illuminated only by the flickering light from the small screen. The smell that permeated the gloom was of ageless dust and decaying fabric, the sepulchral odor of darkness itself.

And in that darkness Fredericks sat without thought, humming soundlessly to himself, waiting.

At 2:30 that afternoon the telephone rang in the study of Winthrop Burnham's country house in Montfort l'Amaury, fifty kilometers to the west of Paris.

As a weekend indulgence, Burnham's housekeeper had made an excellent luncheon—a *gratin de queues d'écrevisses* accompanied by a chilled bottle of Fleurie—and his mood, as he noted the time and picked up the phone, was one of rich content.

"Mr. Burnham?" the familiar voice said, pausing.

"Yes, yes." Burnham said, "Nice to hear from you."

"I'm afraid we have a small problem," the caller said.

"Please go ahead." Burnham was no longer smiling.

"I'm afraid our friend didn't make the plane."

For a moment Burnham was silent. "Have you notified the authorities?"

"No," the caller said, "not yet."

"Good," said Burnham. "Don't. Just have your people pick him up. I'm afraid it's going to have to be his problem, not ours."

"Well, that's not really an option...." Burnham's caller said.

"What do you mean?" said Burnham, his voice

rising. "You have a surveillance team on him, just..."

"He lost the pavement team and made the point man," the caller said, "who is now in postoperative intensive care. No, our friend has gone to ground, and hard."

"Jesus Christ!" Burnham cried, fear turning his lunch to bile.

"Oh, we'll find him," the caller said. "It might take a little time, but we'll find him."

"A little time!" Burnham shouted. "That son of a bitch'll come for me like a shark!"

"Well," Laloux said, "you actually might want to lock your door for a few days. I'll be in touch."

As he stared at the dead phone and tried to breathe normally, Winthrop Burnham's hand began to shake.

ELEVEN

FREDERICKS LEFT THE cinema at four that afternoon. His legs were stiff, and he was conscious of not having eaten. He walked north one block to the place Pigalle and joined the crowd of strollers, who sauntered idly and happily along the boulevard de Rochechouart in the sweet evening air of a Paris Saturday in early spring.

Fredericks strolled with the crowds as far as Barbés-Rochechouart. There he took the No. 4 Métro line, *direction* Montparnasse-Bienvenue, descending and emerging at Saint-Germain-des-Prés.

The tiny place de Furstenburg, on the river side of the Église Saint-Germain-des-Prés, was constructed in the year 1699, by the cardinal whose name it bears, on the site of the old abbey stables. The guide books will tell us that Nos. Six to Eight are the remains of the original construction, and a sign before No. Six will further inform us that it was here that the painter Delacroix had his studio in the nineteenth century.

In summer the square is shaded by the thick leaves of antique paulownia trees, and at evening the soft light from the white-globed gas lamps is diffused and softened among these leaves before it spills, washing gently over the worn cobblestones.

Fredericks entered the mouth of the narrow rue Cardinale, which winds back from the *place* to the boulevard Saint-Germain. Pressing the street button of the first door to his left, he passed into a small and airless courtyard. He ascended a night of worn, stone steps and rang the bell at a heavy, walnut door which bore a small, brass plaque embossed with the initials "E.S."

The door was opened immediately by a young Moroccan boy of astonishing beauty. The boy said nothing, but merely stood and looked at Fredericks, smiling prettily. Behind him, Fredericks could hear shuffling footsteps and recognized the old man's voice. "Maddy, you bitch," the voice wheezed, "when I say I'll get it, that means *don't* you get it!"

With a practiced pout, the boy withdrew into the gloom beyond the door, and his face was replaced with the great, moon face of Edward Stuarti.

"Mr. Pillsbury," the old man said, half-beaming and half-leering, "*long* time, no see."

"Hello, Mary," Fredericks said, smiling.

The door closed behind Fredericks, quickly.

The unprepossessing entranceway and cramped courtyard belied the size of the apartment above. Fredericks walked with Stuarti down the dark hallway toward the glow of the living room, the old man moving awkwardly and supporting his considerable bulk with a black thorn cane.

"How's the arthritis, Mary?" Fredericks asked.

"An utter curse, thank you," Stuarti replied over his shoulder, "visited, *this* season, on my *hips*, courtesy of a sadistic and *tasteless* God. And your good self?"

"In the pink, thanks, Mary," Fredericks replied.

"A pink running to black in the extremities, I notice," Stuarti said.

"You know how hangnails are," Fredericks said.

Stuarti paused, resting against the jamb of the living room door, and regarded Fredericks severely over his glasses. "If I recall correctly, my dear Noah, the very last time I saw you—was it three years ago?—you had a dislocated forefinger and thumbnail that *flapped!*" Stuarti shuddered dramatically. "Perhaps you should consider wearing padded gloves, like the other children who hit each other in the head for a living."

"I don't recall hearing any complaints from you at the time, Mary," Fredericks said.

Stuarti regarded Fredericks. When he spoke his voice was empty of its normal banter.

"None then, dear boy," he said softly, "and none now. I only wish I could have been there to watch."

He was silent as he crossed the room and lowered himself, with considerable effort, into a capacious armchair.

"Drink?" he wheezed.

"A *pastis.*"

"Maddy!" the old man called, and the houseboy reappeared, still pouting. "First," Stuarti said, addressing the boy sternly, "wipe that dreadful expression off your face. Second, bring us the *pastis* tray. Then you may go out and play. Don't come back for an hour."

"I can have a hundred francs?" the boy asked.

"You certainly may *not!*" Stuarti said. "We bought you that shirt on Wednesday. You may take fifty francs."

Fredericks looked about him. The walls of Stuarti's apartment testified to a stubborn love of an earlier age. The near wall was a chaos of paintings, Weimar Berlin predominant; George Grosz, Hannah Hoch. On the south wall, track-lit and beautifully framed, the Augustus John sketch of Oscar Wilde hung alone. The far wall, shelved, was given over to bibelots, folios, dedicated and framed frontispieces, and two perfect shelves of Sèvres and Limoges.

In the old gloom of the apartment, what elsewhere would have been merely the flotsam of a single eccentric life here loomed somehow tragic in the re-created twilight of its own passing.

The boy returned with the cocktail tray. Fredericks served himself, watching the water swirl the amber anise to a smoky-yellow as the sweet licorice odor rose from the glass. From the hall he heard the sound of the front door closing heavily as the boy went out.

"And don't slam the door!" Stuarti turned and beamed at Fredericks. "Lovely, isn't it?"

"Lovely," Fredericks agreed. "Where did you find this one?"

"Micheline DeLage," Stuarti said. "A nasty old bitch, and pricey to boot, but really quite the best procurer of domestics in town."

"You're a perverted old twist, Mary," Fredericks said amiably. "Why can't you take up knitting or whist like the other oldies?"

"My dear boy," Stuarti retorted, "to an artist, regardless of age, the *delectationes* of the senses are quite as essential as the *deliciae* of the spirit."

"And how is the art business, Mary?" Fredericks asked, sipping. "Thriving, I trust?"

"Porcelains and Louis Seize," Stuarti said, with great disgust. "Merchants hedging against inflation while honest painters starve."

"And you?" Fredericks asked.

"Very nicely, thank you," Stuarti giggled. "God bless the Japanese. This year alone I've done a

Chagall study for *David Playing Before Saul,* a Francis Bacon sketch, and a very creditable little Poussin."

"My, my," Fredericks said.

"The provenance for the Poussin is a bit shaky," Stuarti said. "And I was obliged to take some minor short cuts in assembling the palette. The price alone should authenticate it sufficiently, but I still go a bit cold whenever I see an Oriental in the courtyard. And you, my dear Noah? Bring me up to date."

"Oh," Fredericks said, "a little of this, a little of that. Software consulting, mostly."

"Software?" Stuarti arched an eyebrow. "Linens? Leisure suits?"

"Computers, Mary."

"Ah," Stuarti leaned forward and busied himself with the drinks tray. When he looked up, his eyes were sharp.

"Really out, then, are we?" he asked softly.

"Out," Fredericks said. "A long time ago."

"I seem to recall hearing some truly *grim* rumors just after I saw you last," Stuarti said. "Richardson's-Wünderkind-Turns-Werewolf, that sort of thing. *Gothic,* they were. Another drink?"

"Sure," Fredericks said.

"They even got a bit shirty with me," Stuarti said, eyes twinkling, "Seemed to think that I knew something about it. Aiding and abetting, they said, can you imagine? I told Harrison, 'Aiding and abetting, my Aunt Fanny,' I said, 'that's what I get paid for. If someone knows the form and the flavor of the month,' I told him, 'it's hardly my place to ask further questions.' Didn't believe me for a minute. I didn't see another *dollar* from them until Blaine came in as resident, and it's been of-

ficially suggested that I not count too heavily on
any pension."

"I need a few things," Fredericks said.

"I didn't hear that," said Stuarti. "You are an
official bad boy, and the rules against moonlight-
ing are very clear."

"Let's start with names," Fredericks said, "home
team first. Maybe DST, probably SDECE. Last
name Laloux, with an 'X.' No first name. Sixtyish,
maybe a colonel."

"Real name? Work name?" asked Stuarti.

"Work name," Fredericks said.

"Work names are difficult," Stuarti sighed.
"They can be shared, or changed, so file access
alone doesn't make it. Picture?"

"No," said Fredericks.

"Would you recognize a picture?" Stuarti asked.

"Absolutely," Fredericks said.

"Thin," sniffed Stuarti. "I'll see what I can do,
but I shouldn't be too hopeful."

"O.K.," Fredericks said. "Here's an easy one.
Real name and American. Last name Burnham,
first name Winthrop. Also sixtyish. A senior lawyer for Jobert Frères. Ring any bells, that one?"

Stuarti was suddenly silent, brooding over his
drink. When he spoke his voice was leaden.

"My dear boy," he said, not meeting Fredericks's eyes, "let's not have this conversation, shall
we?"

"It's a name to you, is it?" Fredericks pressed.

"A name. That's all."

"Big name?" Fredericks asked. "Little name?
Special name? Above-the-line name? Below-the-
line name? C'mon, Mary! For Christ's sake!"

"Really out, are we?" Stuarti asked mildly.
"Three years isn't much when it comes to deep

cover, after all. Perhaps you could meet me halfway, here?"

"A month or so ago," Fredericks said, "this
Burnham called and asked me to lunch at the
Automobile Club."

"Lucky you." Stuarti was listening very carefully.

"He gave me a transparent cock-and-bull story
about how he got my name, didn't give a damn
whether or not I believed him, and offered me
fifteen grand up front to conduct what amounted
to a dirty title search."

"One assumes," Stuarti said, "that there was a
good reason why they didn't want to do it themselves?"

"Sure," Fredericks said, "it involved a French
politician."

"Ah," Stuarti said. "And you're 'Just-a-Girl-
Who-Can't-Say-No'?"

"Mary," Fredericks said, "I'm not exactly in the
yellow pages, and it's possible that not everyone
I've met has liked me. When someone lies about
how he got my name and dangles fifteen grand in
my face, it behooves me to find out how, and why."

"Yes," Stuarti said, "I suppose it might at that."

"Which I can't do by saying 'no'."

"More *fun* saying 'yes', anyway," Stuarti said.
"Boring, computers, from what I hear...."

"Mary."

"Well, perhaps *fun* isn't the right word, but you
know what I..."

"Shut up," Fredericks said.

"Surely," Stuarti said. "Just thinking aloud,
dear boy."

"The job itself," Fredericks continued, "was

simple enough. I got myself a lawyer, the whole thing took less than forty-eight hours."

"Got?" Stuarti said. "Retained or purchased?"

Fredericks smiled. "That was on the seventh, in and out, neat as you please, absolutely no problem. And on Monday, somebody put the dogs on me, hard."

"Heavy duty for the dogs," Stuarti murmured.

"Two thugs in an Opel Rekord, plus an Algerian baby-sitter on the street. It was set up beforehand, so they knew where I lived, and they came right for me, so they must have had pictures."

"Oops," said Stuarti.

"Now either the Algerian had more connections than Kissinger, or the whole incident was a rather elaborate piece of theater, staged at his considerable expense, because I hadn't even gotten my hands washed before half the *flics* in Paris came through the front door with riot guns and put me in irons."

"That was this Monday?!" Stuarti asked sharply.

"Relax, Mary," Fredericks said. "Let me finish."

"Shit!" Stuarti said. "Shit!"

"First night at the Commissariat Saint-Gervais, private room. I never saw the booking charges. Next day, transferred to a transit detention center in the place Saint-Honoré. Private room again, still no booking charges, still no attempt to put together the formal statement.

"Third night," Fredericks continued, "this is Wednesday now, our friend Laloux and some of his SDECE boys show up, and over the next thirty-six hours we tape an interrogation. Only thing is, it's *not* an interrogation. He doesn't give a damn about the baby-sitter and there's nothing I could have told him about myself that he didn't already know. It seemed more a process of reading my dossier into the record than anything else...."

"My dear boy," Stuarti shifted in his chair, "it's getting late...."

"Which forces one to re-examine some earlier assumptions. First, I assumed that Burnham offered me the job because he, or his firm, didn't want to do it. Let's assume, instead, that someone wanted *me*, specifically, to do it."

"Noah...."

"Shut up. Second, I assumed at first that whoever put the dogs on me wanted to warn me off. Let's assume instead that they wanted me to kick the dogs, the harder the better. Third, I assumed that I was arrested for dog-kicking and prying into the affairs of French politicians. Which assumption falls *all* apart if they have no intention of prosecuting."

"What do you mean?" Stuarti asked.

"Yesterday afternoon," Fredericks said, "they put me back on the street. On a short leash, with some baby-sitters, a one-way ticket to New York, and the firm advice that I leave France while it's still an option."

"*Good* advice," Stuarti said "*wise* counsel...."

"Mary," said Fredericks, "the flight left this afternoon."

"Oh, Jesus Christ!" Stuarti groaned. "Am I to understand that, *A*, you're hot in this country, and *B*, you're sitting in *my* living room! Is that what you're telling me?"

"Burnham," Fredericks prompted. "Your turn, Mary."

"Let's do the rest by phone, shall we?" Stuarti

struggled forward in his chair. "Leave me a number, I'll get back...."

"No," Fredericks said, smiling.

Stuarti regarded Fredericks's smile, and then the pale, blue eyes that so flatly contradicted it.

"I have a friend," Stuarti said slowly, "who gets his hair cut at the Embassy. The chatty old loony with the little barber shop up on the second floor, you know it, right?"

"Sure."

"Well, so does our friend Burnham. Now, you'll recall the layout, you get to the top of the stairs, and there's the wire-service ticker and newspaper room to the right, and the barber shop down toward the end of the hall to the left, O.K.?"

"Go ahead."

"Now if you keep *on* to the left," Stuarti said, "you come to another set of stairs, which go directly from the second to the fourth floor. And that's where you *stop,* because those stairs have floor-to-ceiling mesh doors and two Marines at each end, with photographs on clipboards."

Fredericks raised his eyebrows.

"Communications," Stuarti said shortly. "The high-speed squirt-and-fancy phone boys. That's also where they prepare the bag."

"And Burnham?"

"A fastidious groomer, it would appear," Stuarti said. "Gets his hair cut at least once a week, sometimes more. The funny thing is, my friend says he always turns the wrong way out of the barber shop."

"Weak sense of direction, maybe?"

"Must be," Stuarti said. "Must have those Marines bamboozled, too, seems they let him through every time."

In the silence the ticking of the ormolu clock on Stuarti's mantel seemed suddenly amplified.

"If one didn't know better," Fredericks said, "it'd sound like the bastard's a spook."

"Impossible," Stuarti said. "We would have seen his name in *Le Canard*. Nope, just a simple lawyer, I'd say."

"With access to, and thus presumably the need for, high-speed and high-security communications gear?"

"That's it," Stuarti said.

"And how's his access to the resident?" asked Fredericks. "Blaine know him?"

"Got me," Stuarti said flatly. "I'm a painter."

"I'll need some walking-around papers, Mary." Fredericks poured himself another drink.

"Money time, darling," Stuarti said. "We all have to pay the rent. That going to be a problem?"

"How about a check?" Fredericks smiled.

"Sure," Stuarti said, "for a check, let's see, I could do you a nice British, an Ulster Catholic say, in the fertilizer business, buying phosphates on the continent. I'll throw in an IRA lapel pin for free."

Fredericks laughed and removed a thick envelope from his suit pocket, which he passed to Stuarti.

Stuarti opened the envelope and contemplated for a moment the hundred-franc notes that it contained. He removed five of the notes and returned the envelope to Fredericks.

"Cost-price for you, dear boy," Stuarti said. "Can you run a Belgian?"

"Sure."

"Congratulations," Stuarti said. "You are now

an accountant from Liège. More specifically, since we have no pictures, you are an accountant from Liège who has left his passport in his hotel room."

"Fine," Fredericks said. "Listen, Mary. I'll probably be wanting a full set of French. Custom. When I know the name I'll let you know. They won't be used in this country."

Stuarti shrugged. "Your money. I'll get the papers." He rose laboriously and shuffled out of the room.

When Stuarti returned to the living room Fredericks was standing, regarding the Augustus John sketch. Stuarti addressed his back.

"We both believe in the sanctity of a loyalty given, dear boy, which makes us as anachronistic as the giant lizards of the Mesozoic, and very nearly as vulnerable. I'm in your debt, and I'll do what I can to help you, but you must remember—I'm just a housemother, and an old man into the bargain. Don't ask for more than I have to give."

Fredericks turned and took the envelope.

"I'll be in touch," he said.

Outside, the night was chill and cloudless. The sky, above the low buildings, had deepened to a darker, more trembling, blue. Fredericks walked to the place Saint-Germain, passed the Deux Magots and the Flore, and crossed against the traffic into the narrow rue du Dragon.

The restaurant was high-ceilinged and brightly lit from above by large electric bar lights, which made it easy to read while one ate.

Before Fredericks had known Danielle, he had regularly taken his evening meals there. Afterward, he had come there less. With its bright lights, its paper place mats, its plastic table tops and cruets, it was not a restaurant for couples. Danielle had objected to the proprietary familiarity with which the three old ladies who ran the restaurant had treated Fredericks, and they, being hard-headed women from the Midi, had regarded her beauty with overt suspicion.

"Monsieur Noah!" the old lady exclaimed, scurrying to greet Fredericks. "It's been too long. Things go well?"

"Madame Odile," Fredericks said, bowing elegantly over her hand, "more lovely than ever."

Blushing furiously and giggling, the old lady led Fredericks to the corner table he had always favored, a table that commanded a view both of the door and of the kitchen. Affection expressed, the other ladies greeted, and mutual news and health reports exchanged, Madame Odile asked him, eyes already twinkling in anticipation, what he would have that evening.

It was a joke of long standing, based on the fact that Fredericks was American.

"*Voyons*," Fredericks said gravely, "*auriez-vous, peut-être, un* Morton's Hungry-Man Beefsteak Dinner, *avec un demi* Diet Pepsi?"

"Impossible!" the old lady cried with delight. "But what could it be?"

As Fredericks explained, she was forced to clap her hand over her mouth to suppress her giggling. Cries of outrage and delight followed her return to the kitchen.

Fredericks was given a beautiful *daube de lapin*, the delicate meat simmering in an exquisite red wine sauce, accompanied by sweet green beans with almond slivers and a large carafe of Cahors. He finished his meal with a fresh *crème caramel*,

111

two espressos, and a large Calvados for which he was not allowed to pay.

He had been very hungry, and the food was very good.

Leaving the restaurant, Fredericks walked to *Le Drugstore* at Saint-Germain-des-Prés. There he purchased a toothbrush and toothpaste, razor, shaving cream, comb, deodorant, and a bottle of Johnny Walker whisky.

From there he walked up the rue de Rennes toward Montparnasse, carrying his purchases in a paper bag.

The hotel he selected was one of many in the shabby side streets behind the Gare Montparnasse. The lobby was empty when Fredericks entered.

The night clerk, who resembled a weasel were weasels prone to stain their teeth and fingertips with nicotine, looked up as the door banged sharply open, and then he rose quickly to his feet. Fredericks, in an expensive suit and overcoat, did not look like the hotel's normal custom.

Fredericks crossed to the desk, placed his paper bag on it, and set the unopened bottle of Johnny Walker, which he now carried in his fist, next to the paper bag, hard.

"Sir?" the desk clerk asked, nervously.

Fredericks regarded him for a moment before he spoke.

"I want a room," Fredericks said.

"Sir?" the desk clerk said.

"A room," Fredericks said. "With a bed, a bathroom, a glass, some ice, and a minimum of conversation. This is a hotel, is it not?"

"Yes, sir," the desk clerk said. "We have a room

with a private toilet, sir, the bath is separate. Forty francs a night, five for..."

Fredericks held up his hand. "Fine." He removed a hundred-franc note from his pocket and threw it onto the desk. "Keep it," he said. "And get me some ice."

Thus when the desk clerk asked for identification, his heart was not really in it.

"Identify?" Fredericks said, slightly slurring his excellent French and fixing the clerk with a smile of clenched fury. "A fascinating question, let's see, who am I? I am the husband of a faithless wife, the purchaser of groceries for ungrateful children, the mortgage-holder of the fine home in which they live and in which, God willing, they will all die rapid and inexpensive deaths, and the proud owner of..." Fredericks opened his paper bag "...a new toothbrush, razor, deodorant, and comb. Where is the goddamned key?"

In the exercise of that indulgence granted often by the French to large domestic sorrows, and always to large tips, the desk clerk indicated that the registration card could wait until morning.

TWELVE

WINTHROP BURNHAM WAS picked up on the Champs-Elysées as he left the Traveller's Club where, each Thursday, he took his lunch.

It was very unobtrusively done.

As Burnham left the entranceway of the Traveller's Club and eased into the midday pedestrian traffic, two young men in suits—clearly businessmen or bureaucrats—suddenly appeared at either elbow. Burnham was addressed, politely, by name. The taller of the two men removed a wallet from his jacket pocket and stood at Burnham's side, smiling as though sharing snapshots of children as Burnham verified the identification.

The Citröen to which they led Burnham idled quietly at the curb before the Gaumont-Elysées Cinéma. It was black, which in France is the color of officialdom.

In the car the men were silent and had no answers to Burnham's irritated and nervous questions. They crossed the river at the Pont Alexandre III and moments later pulled to the curb in the rue Saint-Dominique, at the rear of the massive building that houses the offices of the Defense Ministry. Leaving the car in a restricted parking zone, they entered the building through a very unimposing street-level door, passed two security desks without offering any identification, and took a service elevator to the third floor.

The office into which Burnham was shown was unprepossessing, as was, at first glance, the balding man behind the desk who rose courteously when Burnham entered.

"Winthrop Burnham?" the man asked, almost apologetically.

"Yes," Burnham snapped, betraying no recognition at all, "and who the hell are you, and what's this all about?"

"Leave us, please," Laloux said to the two young men.

As the door closed behind Laloux's adjutants, Burnham cleared his throat to speak. Laloux silenced him with a raised hand and pointed to the ceiling. From a capacious briefcase on the floor Laloux removed what appeared to be a small portable tape recorder. When he depressed the "play" key, the recorder emitted a sudden and startling babble of voices, simultaneously speaking gibberish in what seemed at least a dozen languages.

"I'm sorry I couldn't forewarn you, Mr. Burnham," he said, across the cacophony, "but doing so would have entailed needless risk."

"Once again," Burnham said, breathing out heavily, "you have succeeded in turning an excellent lunch to bile. What is that godawful noise?"

"It's called a babbler," Laloux said, smiling with pride. "Kissinger writes about it in his memoirs."

"Wonderful," Burnham said sourly. "Yet another marvel of twentieth-century statecraft. How the hell are you supposed to hear yourself think?"

"It was used by the Nixon White House on the China trips," Laloux said.

"Of course," Burnham said, nodding.

Laloux's smile was noticeably frosty as the two men regarded one another with mutual antipathy. "Any calls you have to make, Mr. Burnham?" he asked. "Any appointments to clear? We'll probably need about two hours here."

Using the desk phone, Burnham rang his secretary and ordered that his afternoon appointments be rescheduled.

"Well, so far, so good," Laloux said, when Burnham had hung up, though it was not clear from his voice whether he was congratulating Burnham or merely rehearsing the idiom. "Shall we see where we are?

"First, we now have a clearly documented run, by an equally clearly documented American agent, at a prominent French politician. Second, contrary to our earlier fears, Mr. Fredericks was *most* forthcoming, and supplied your name as his case officer at the first request."

"Surely he didn't say 'case officer'?" Burnham objected.

"Not in those words, of course," Laloux agreed, "but the implication is clear enough that your corroboration on tape will cement it."

"All right," Burnham said. "Go ahead."

"Your name was then removed from the tape transcripts, and cross-referenced to an internal file of the highest classification, all access through me."

Burnham nodded.

"This afternoon," Laloux continued, "we will tie up our little knot with the formal—taped—'Turning of Winthrop Burnham,' in which a high-level, below-the-line Agency resident, yourself, is caught supervising the compromise of a French politician, and enjoying neither diplomatic immunity nor the thought of a career-ending scandal, is persuaded to be turned and played back in exchange for our silence."

"O capricious fates!" Burnham murmured. "An illustrious, if dual, career, cruelly burked in its gentle twilight."

"The fact that I have always insisted on running my own doubles has two distinct advantages," Laloux continued, frowning slightly. "The first of these is that it will allow us to meet clandestinely without arousing suspicion on behalf of my service...."

"Perhaps somewhat *less* clandestinely in the future," Burnham said, "it's hell on my angina."

"At these meetings," Laloux continued, clearly more interested in modalities than in Burnham's heart, "you will arrange to supply me with hardcopy chickenfood of a quality adequate to sustain your identity as a high-level double. This *must* not be garbage, Mr. Burnham. It is my only protection, and without it I am naked. Be sure that your people understand this, and understand further that I will know the difference."

"Chickenfeed," Burnham said.

"Pardon?" Laloux said, sharply.

"Chickenfeed," Burnham said, "not 'chickenfood'."

"The second advantage," Laloux continued after a moment of cold silence, "is that I shall be able, immediately, to put men both on your car and on your home."

"I'm not sure I see the advantage to that," Burnham said.

"For the next few days, perhaps," Laloux said, no longer looking directly at Burnham, "it would seem a prudent safeguard."

Burnham sat up sharply. "Are you trying to tell me that you still don't have Fredericks in custody?"

"A matter of days," Laloux shrugged, still not meeting Burnham's eye, "*if* he is still in France."

"Goddamn it!" Burnham cried. "That's an unacceptable 'if'!"

"Mr. Burnham," Laloux said with some anger, "it was your people who proposed Mr. Fredericks for the role of sacrificial lamb, and your people who insisted, with uncharacteristic and lamentable sentimentality, that he live. Please direct any reproaches you may now have to them."

"Listen to me," Burnham said, speaking slowly to give weight to his urgency. "Until you have that son of a bitch locked up, you keep your people *close*, do you understand? Further, should Mr. Fredericks be killed resisting arrest, I would report it as a necessary operational contingency for which I would assume full responsibility, is that clear?

"You'll be covered by my best people, Mr. Burnham. I don't think you need to..."

"Is that clear?" Burnham repeated, and it was very much an order.

"As you like," Laloux shrugged.

"You have something for me" Burnham was still upset.

Laloux regarded Burnham thoughtfully for a moment, and then removed a small, black, film cassette from his jacket pocket.

"Our most recent internal estimates of Chinese submarine capacity," he said to Burnham, handing him the cassette. "Han class and G-2s. I'll expect confirmation of the deposit from Zurich within four days."

Burnham pocketed the cassette. "One question, Colonel, if I may?"

"Certainly."

"If the files are to show me doubled," said Burnham slowly, "it occurs to me that they will also show it to have been properly done, that is, both burned *and* bribed. Might one safely assume that that nonaccountable budgetary supplement is being added monthly to your account?"

Laloux smiled. "Are you ready to make the tape now, Mr. Burnham?"

"I only ask," Burnham continued, "to remind you that whatever happens to me, happens to that supplement. You keep your people *close*."

Laloux stopped the babbler, plunging them into a blessed silence, and replaced it in his briefcase. He then rose and crossed to the door. Opening it, he spoke into the corridor.

"Phillipe," he said, "would you and Jean-Claude come in, please, and bring the tape recorder."

THIRTEEN

FREDERICKS LEFT THE hotel early the next morning. From Montparnasse he took the Métro to the flea market at Clingancourt in the north of Paris. At an elegant *antiquaire* in the Marché Biron he exchanged his Swiss francs for French in a marginally advantageous (and entirely undocumented) transaction. From a sidewalk vendor he purchased a well-traveled leather suitcase, and in the course of two hours' idle shopping assembled an unremarkable wardrobe of unlabeled factory seconds with which to fill it.

By two in the afternoon he had returned to the seventh arrondissement and, using the Belgian identity papers with which Stuarti had provided him, was registered in a small hotel in the rue de Bac.

Fredericks's hotel room fronted on the street, and, from a *boulangerie* beneath, the sweet, yeasty smells of the afternoon's baking rose to his window as he sat at the room's small desk.

From his suit-coat pocket Fredericks removed a United States airmail envelope and a plain sheet of white bond. He addressed the envelope in a neat hand:

> *Mr. Winthrop Burnham*
> *c/o Jobert Frères*
> *16, Avenue George V*
> *Paris, 75008*
> *FRANCE*

Dear Mr. Burnham, (he wrote)

*At our initial meeting on 25 March, I
expressed to you my concern that inquiries
into the financial affairs of M. Jean-Jacques
Cassin might, should they come to light, be
easily subject to misinterpretation.*

*Such concern, unfortunately, has proven well
founded.*

*On the evening of 19 April I was arrested at
my home by French security police and
accused of conspiring to subvert M. Cassin
through blackmail. This charge, coupled with
other contingencies which need not concern
you, has resulted in my de facto deportation
from France.*

*My arrest was accompanied by the seizure of
many of my personal papers; among these was
my (uncashed) retainer check from Jobert
Frères.*

*I write now to request that you stop payment
on this lost check and, as expeditiously as
possible, forward the funds concerned (U. S.
$15,000) to my account: c/o Marine Midland
Bank, 437 Madison Avenue, New York, NY
10022, A/C No. 017 1452 8.*

*I trust that I may depend on your honor in
this regard as you may depend on my
continued discretion.*

> *Sincerely,*

Fredericks reread the letter, smiled, and sealed it. On a second sheet of paper he jotted a brief note to an old friend living in New York.

Dear Jack, (he wrote)

Would you mail the enclosed from New York ASAP? Letter follows.

Best,

Noah

At a *tabac* on the corner of the rue de Varenne Fredericks purchased the necessary postage and mailed the note, with the letter to Burnham enclosed, to his friend's New York address.

Fredericks took dinner late that evening, for the *quartier* that was his destination only comes to life around eleven.

He left the hotel at 10:30, taking the Métro from the Odéon to Réaumur-Sébastopol. He wore an ill-fitting wool suit and a clip-on necktie that he had purchased that afternoon at the flea market.

He dined at an inexpensive *brasserie* on the boulevard Sébastopol. He ate only soup and a small steak and drank mineral water with his meal. After dinner, still waiting, he had two coffees and watched the pinball jockeys as they slapped the machines, cursing and cajoling through their cigarettes.

At 11:30 he settled his check and stepped into the street outside. The night air, though chilly, was heavy, and the street smelled of exhaust fumes and fried potatoes. He walked one block west to the rue Saint-Denis, into which he turned, walking north.

The pedestrian traffic was almost wholly male. Small knots of men stood here and there before dimly lit doorways, staring silently at the prostitutes who stood inside, smiling, taunting, beckoning. The streetwalkers who were visible were those catering exclusively to masochists, leaning insolently against the walls in crotch-length leather skirts, cracking riding crops against their military boots and glaring, in hope of custom, at the men who scurried by.

Two blocks north, toward the Porte Saint-Denis, Fredericks turned into the narrow rue Blondel. Here were located the small, expensive bars that served the carriage trade of the *quartier,* where one could sit over an overpriced and overwatered whisky and make one's selection at leisure from younger, fresher stock.

Fredericks entered a bar marked only by a small *placque* on its door as *Chez Blondine.* An elegantly dressed hostess bade him good evening and explained, in a discreet voice, that *Chez Blondine* was a private club, in which, however, guest membership could be arranged for an honorarium of 20 francs.

Such arrangement accomplished, Fredericks passed from the reception area and joined his fellow members in the bar. The room was carpeted and illuminated by indirect rose lighting. There was a small bar with half-a-dozen high banquettes and a number of small tables with comfortable chairs spaced discreetly apart along the wall. A Johnny Mathis tape was playing softly.

At the table nearest the entranceway to the bar, a sweating and heavy-set German murmured endearments, in execrable French, to a lovely young red-haired girl who smiled and pouted and played with his shirt buttons as he spoke. It was the only table occupied—explained, Fredericks reflected, more by the fact of the hour than that of the Sabbath.

There were three girls at the bar, carefully dressed and coiffed to sustain the illusion of elegance, an illusion not altogether aided by the barman's antique tuxedo. As Fredericks sipped his drink, the girl nearest to him slid from her stool and began to dance softly to the music.

Her hair was blond and long, and her skin was deeply tanned. She wore a low-cut and backless white dress, beneath which she was clearly naked. For a moment she gave Fredericks her back and hips to watch, then turned and smiled, her hips still stirring to the music.

"Tu danses?" she asked.

"It's more serious than that, I'm afraid," Fredericks replied, smiling back.

The girl laughed, dancing closer. "How serious, *chéri?*" she asked, sipping from Fredericks's glass and smiling at him over the rim.

"Grave," Fredericks said, "very grave. A case for immediate attention."

"Expensive," the girl said, lifting her hair from the nape of her neck with both hands in a gesture that raised her lovely breasts taut against the thin fabric of her dress, "such attention."

"Doubtless," Fredericks said.

"Two hundred and fifty francs," the girl said, still smiling.

"Impressive," Fredericks said.

"And worth it," the girl said, running her fingernail down Fredericks's thigh.

Fredericks paid the barman as the girl got her coat.

Together they crossed the street to a small hotel, more presentable than most in the area. A sign inside the door read *"Complet."*

The girl removed a key from her coat pocket and opened the door. The reception desk was on the second floor. There were two men behind the desk, one old, one young. The old man wordlessly handed the girl two towels and a key. The young man sat in a propped-back chair with his feet against the desk. He was small and dark-complexioned, with black hair slicked back and heavily pomaded. He wore a loud and over-large sports jacket. He briefly raised his eyes from the sex magazine he was reading, regarded Fredericks with incurious contempt, then returned his attention to the pictures.

The room, just down the hall from the desk, had only a bed, a chair, a sink, and an empty armoire. The bulb in the bedside lamp, already on, was rose.

The girl locked the door behind them, then turned to Fredericks and smiled. She slipped the straps of the dress from her shoulders and let it drop to the floor.

Naked, she was lovely.

"You, too," she said and stepped from the dress.

"Listen," Fredericks said in an uneasy voice, "that little *mec* at the desk had a gun under his jacket. I saw it."

The girl smiled at him over her shoulder as she hung her dress in the armoire.

130

"Only for protection of the guests, *chéri*. You have nothing to worry about here."

"Are you sure you locked the door?" Fredericks asked, very much the nervous out-of-towner worried about being robbed.

"Check it for yourself, *chéri*." The girl crossed to the sink.

Fredericks fiddled briefly with the lock and saw there what he knew he would. The flange into which the bolt was passed was mounted on a strip of soft molding. At the least pressure it would come right off the wall.

The girl was at the sink, bending to fill a small basin with warm water. Fredericks stroked her smooth young back, his hand trailing to her buttocks. She cocked her hips and parted her legs slightly, and a silky tendril of her pubic tuft brushed his palm. Fredericks's fingers traced the line of her buttock to the place where it became the soft skin of her inner thigh.

Which sweetest of sweet meats, with deep regret and regrettable force, he pinched.

The girl went off like a factory shift whistle.

"Eeyow!" she screamed, leaping into the air as the basin clattered to the floor. "Gaëtan!"

Fredericks pressed himself against the wall next to the door.

The little bouncer who came bursting through the door, gun already dangling from his hand, never even saw him.

Fredericks hit him with a two-knuckle punch in the temple, taking him off his feet sideways. He was unconscious before he hit the floor.

The girl filled her lungs to scream again. Fredericks shook his head and held his finger to his lips. The girl's mouth shut abruptly.

Fredericks knelt and picked up the gun. It was a Walther 9 mm. automatic. The chamber was empty and the clip was full.

Fredericks checked the safety, then tucked the gun into the back of his belt, beneath the poorly fitting suit coat. He then removed a roll of hundred-franc notes from his pants pocket. Peeling off three of these, he turned to the naked girl, who stood with one hand clapped to her mouth and the other to her bottom.

"I'm sorry, darling," he said. "Find someone with a pistol for sale these days, it's six-to-five you're talking to a cop. Rub these on the bruise."

Gingerly the girl took the proffered bills.

Fredericks glanced at the little hoodlum on the floor. His left leg was rigid and quivering and a thin trickle of blood issued from his ear.

"Now here's what *you* do," Fredericks said to the girl. "First, you sit down in the chair."

The girl sat down, quickly.

"Then," Fredericks said, "you count to two hundred, slowly, and when you're finished, you call a doctor for your little chaperon there, *compris?*"

The girl nodded, eyes wide.

"No cheating, now," Fredericks smiled, "you're going to count *slowly,* right?"

The girl nodded vigorously.

"Goodbye, darling," Fredericks said. "You're a beauty."

The old man stood stolidly at the reception desk, his attention firmly fixed on the newspaper before him.

Fredericks wished him good evening as he left.

* * *

By twelve-fifteen Fredericks was again in his hotel room overlooking the rue de Bac.

Although he had struck with his right hand, the broken little finger of his left hand had been inadvertently jarred or clenched, and new swelling now caused it to ache with a dull insistence in which he could feel the beat of his heart.

He filled the room's small sink with cold water and sat quietly, soaking it. He drank vodka from the tooth-glass, replenishing it occasionally from a bottle that stood on the glass shelf above the sink.

The girl—her nakedness—had stirred him, and as he sat at the basin he had to force himself not to think. Such emptying of emotion was normally a practiced discipline.

He looked at his shoes and thought of shoes. He looked at the floor and imagined push-ups. Refilling his glass, he read everything on the vodka bottle. The vodka, he noticed, was Polish.

And suddenly, utterly unbidden, he recalled an incident cited somewhere in a book by Adam Ulam on the early period of the Cold War. It concerned, he remembered vaguely, the founding conference of the United Nations, at which Poland, unexpectedly, was not represented. Pressed by his British and American colleagues, V. M. Molotov had finally admitted that the Polish resistance leaders were under detention in the Soviet Union for unspecified crimes.

It was less the material incident, however, that the Polish vodka now brought to mind, than Molotov's reply to a query concerning the Poles' eventual fate.

"The guilty," he is said to have replied gravely, "will be tried."

It began as a soft chuckle, then became laughter that shook him, and then something else that shook him and that he could not stop.

He stood abruptly, breathing deeply and trying to force himself to yawn. After a while, the shaking stopped.

Fredericks extinguished the light and lay, still clothed, on the narrow bed. The room was dimly illuminated by the lights from the street. Cars passed occasionally, always at high speed. The vodka bottle was near his hand on the floor, and the night air from the open window was cool on his wet face.

Fredericks's normal companion for serious vodka drinking during the past three years had been, like Mr. Molotov, Russian.

The card on the door of her tiny apartment on the third floor of Danielle's ancient building identified its occupant as a Madame Chaliapin, and gave as her profession *Traducteuse*.

From time to time, a hyphen would appear after Madame Chaliapin's last name, followed (in Fredericks's tenure) by such names as Mayakovsky, Andreyev, Scriabin, and Diaghilev, suggesting to Fredericks and Danielle that her identity lay more firmly in period than in profession.

Indeed, they had never known her to have a job of translation, busy as she was intriguing by post to recover a patrimony stolen during the October Revolution, journeying twice weekly to the *quartier de Gergovie* to buy black bread, and otherwise lamenting, with Pope Gregory, that her soul should be forced to engage in the business of the world, and thus be defiled in the dirt of earthly corruption.

The people of the neighborhood considered her a lunatic.

Fredericks and Danielle, to whose affections elderly emigré ladies had easy access, were quite fond of her indeed.

Perhaps once a month Madame Chaliapin would knock at their door, bearing black bread as a gift. Often, by happy coincidence, Fredericks would have a bottle of chilled vodka in the refrigerator and, with considerable effort, would be able to prevail upon Madame Chaliapin to accept a glass or three.

At their first meeting, Madame Chaliapin had been largely impressed by Fredericks's books; accounting him by their number a wise man (a classic example, Fredericks reflected, of facts underdetermining theory). Political discussion is the inevitable product obtained when vodka is added to elderly *emigrés* and Madame Chaliapin was a direct woman.

"Vous êtes communiste?" she had asked belligerently.

No, Fredericks had answered, no, he wasn't.

"Ah, vous êtes donc anticommuniste?"

Fredericks had answered more slowly here, finally observing that given the fact that in sixty years communism had only succeeded in producing police states, and that the Soviet Union was unable to feed itself, that anticommunism, while laudable, seemed at best a part-time political preoccupation.

"But then," Madame Chaliapin had asked, gesturing at the books on the shelves, "what is it, your political belief?"

It was Danielle who had answered, giggly with vodka.

"It's simple," she had said, "Read and Let Read."

Later, when Madame Chaliapin had gone, Fredericks had offered Danielle, in return for her observation, a practical demonstration of another maxim of political theory: that a Prince must rule through *amour et cremeur*, love and fear.

The fear part was very easy, Danielle being extremely ticklish, and the love part easier still.

Winthrop Burnham's large apartment was in Auteuil, in the southern portion of the elegant sixteenth arrondissement. The apartment was one of twelve in an eight-story contemporary residential building in the manicured rue de l'Yvette.

Though formally and expensively furnished, the apartment lacked what Burnham, never having been married, formulated as "warmth" and was used only during the week as a pied-à-terre. The weekends, preferring the comforts of his country house and the admirable cuisine of the local woman who prepared his meals, he invariably spent at Montfort l'Amaury.

It was Burnham's habit each morning to drive to work, taking the right-bank quais to the place de l'Alma and up the avenue George V to his office. This sunny April morning, however, Burnham left his apartment building on foot. The air was light and warm and liquor-sweet with the soft smell of earth, which in Paris accompanies the change of seasons. That it was sunny and spring, alas, had very little to do with his decision.

Burnham stepped into the street at 9:15.

The early flowers in the carefully tended strip

of garden in front of his building were colorful and gay in the morning sun. In the small park across the street, already swelling to a brighter green, babies played and *au pairs* chatted, and an elegantly suited old man, with polished cane and boutonniere, sat quietly on a bench, his obligatory *Le Monde* folded in his lap; his blood, like the city's, warming in the new sun.

Although Laloux's two bodyguards changed in a four-hour rotation, the cars in which they sat, thirty meters to either side of Burnham's building, did not. By the time Burnham reached the sidewalk and turned left, walking slowly toward the avenue Mozart, both men had left and locked their cars—a battered Simca 1100 and a new gray Peugeot sedan—and were with him, one in front and one behind. The men—one young, one less young—were unremarkable both of dress and feature, and only their empty hands and watcher's eyes might have hinted at their profession.

The Métro station—its name, *Jasmin,* in happy harmony with the perfect morning—was just at the end of the street. The rush hour over, there were few people.

Burnham purchased a *carnet* of ten first-class tickets and entered onto the platform marked *direction Montreuil*. One of his sitters was already on the platform ahead of him. The other followed. They did not look at one another.

The train hissed to a stop, and Burnham entered the yellow first-class compartment. There, in the company of three elegantly dressed older women and one (no less elegantly dressed) little girl, Burnham rode one stop to the Métro station Ranelagh.

Emerging into the rue du Ranelagh, Burnham

paused at the curb. One of his sitters walked past him and crossed the street. He could not see the other. A black Citröen glided noiselessly to the curb in front of him. Burnham opened the passenger door and entered the car. As he closed the door behind him and the car left the curb, Laloux wished him a good morning.

Laloux drove east toward the Seine at a leisurely pace. When he suddenly accelerated at a group of schoolchildren outside the Lycée Molière, scattering them, like pigeons, unhurt to either side, it was clearly a matter of that national obligation incumbent upon French drivers rather than any actual urgency.

It was Burnham who spoke first.

"We assume, Colonel, that you are in receipt of the funds?"

"Why, yes," Laloux said, "yes. And I trust that your people were pleased with the product?"

"Delighted," Burnham said. "And may I further assume, from the continuing fact of your thugs outside my home, that Fredericks has yet to be picked up?"

"They are not thugs," said Laloux. "Two, in fact, are graduates of the École Normale d'Administration."

"Actually," Burnham replied, "I'd *prefer* thugs."

"The woman," Laloux said after a pause, "is being watched. We have people both on her and on her phone there. So far, nothing. Also her apartment, her bank, his bank. Nothing. The woman has given instructions for his mail to be forwarded, care of his bank in New York. You haven't heard from him?"

"No," Burnham said, "thank Christ."

"We do the hotel *fiches* daily. Also hospitals, prisons, hostels, the whole routine. The police are looking, too, although they don't know quite what for, save a name. And none of his clients have heard from him, as best as we can determine. Normally, we would assume him gone."

They turned onto the quai by the Maison de l'ORTF, the headquarters of the state-run broadcasting services. The traffic was light as they drove along the river.

"If he *is* in Paris," Laloux said, "I believe we may safely assume that he is *not* using his own identity papers. Did he, to your knowledge, ever run other identities than those indicated in the file?"

"I've no idea," Burnham said. "You've read the same file I have."

"How about local access to papers?" Laloux asked. "Is there anyone to whom he might go here?"

"I don't know," Burnham said. "I can ask."

They crossed the river at the Pont d'Iéna, Trocadéro at their back and the Eiffel tower soaring before them. As they turned onto the Quai de Grenelle a second Citröen, this one dark red, turned with them. It had been behind them on the opposite bank. Laloux spoke before Burnham could ask.

"Mine," he said. "And it would be helpful if I had something to justify the use of such manpower."

Burnham opened his briefcase on his lap and removed a manilla envelope, which he placed on the seat between them.

"Organization chart of Paris station," he said, "a summary of Brief, and the internal courier lines in the *bassin Parisien*."

"Shit!" Laloux said. "For such things I buy a secretary, not a resident case officer."

"It's supposed to be a first bite, my friend, not the Allied Order of Battle."

"It has to be better next time," Laloux said, "or I will not continue."

"I'll tell them. You have something for me?"

Laloux removed two film cassettes from his suit-coat pocket, placing them on top of the manilla envelope. "First cassette. A summary of Soviet-French discussions of joint armaments production. The talks, held in Rambouillet from 21 January to 4 February, were nominally concerned with negotiating a distribution agreement between Hotchkiss-Brandt and the KAMA Purchasing Commission. In fact, they were bilateral negotiations on joint production."

"Names?" Burnham pocketed the cassette.

"There's a list of both delegations," Laloux said. "Second cassette, all nonpublic notes and codicils to the negotiations, also current."

"Excellent." Burnham took the second cassette.

"It is," Laloux agreed. "It's also a double, for which I will expect double payment."

"I'm not sure I understand."

"It's very easy," Laloux said. "The notes and codicils were cross-referenced only in the summary. Obtaining them required that I access a second file, and take a second set of pictures. I assume, Mr. Burnham, that you wanted the notes and codicils?"

"Yes," Burnham said, "yes."

"Good," Laloux said. "And perhaps we can avoid future semantic difficulties by adopting a working definition of what, precisely, constitutes a double product, yes?"

"Such as?"

"If I say it does," Laloux said, "it does. I'll expect confirmation of the funds by Monday next."

Laloux dropped Burnham in the rue du Docteur-Blanche, at the opposite end of the rue de l'Yvette from the Métro Jasmin. The burgundy Citröen, its window glass smoked, paused briefly as it glided by Burnham, and he registered a sharp twinge of professional distaste as he realized that he was being photographed. The entire exchange, from the time he had left his front door to the time he was returned to it, had taken thirty-five minutes.

The bodyguard in the Simca 1100 did not even look up as Burnham passed on the sidewalk, turned, and entered his building.

In the sweet spring the flowers drank the sun, the children gaily played, and only the elegant old man remained to foretell mortality as, gathering his newspaper and straightening his boutonniere, Stuarti rose on his cane and passed slowly from the park, his step fettered by age and the arthritis in his hips.

FOURTEEN

THE WEATHER HELD, the exquisite days of mild, intoxicating warmth, the evenings of a beauty infinitely gentle; a season for langourous luncheons in *jardins fleuris* and love beneath new stars.

Alas, it was instead to archives that Fredericks's homework consigned him, as he began his search for the nameless brother of a faceless member of the Chambre des Députés.

Fredericks began his homework in the Bibliothèque de l'Arsenal, the large municipal library situated in the boulevard Morland in the fourth arrondissement. The fruit of a morning's research was meager; while the references both to Entreprises Cassin and to its nineteenth-century founder, Georges Cassin, were numerous, the record, with respect to his great-grandsons, was reticent. Indeed, the only direct reference came in an edition of *Le Figaro* following the most recent elections to the National Assembly, in which the newly elected Deputies were listed with a brief following line of biography. This informed Fredericks that Jean-Jacques Cassin had been born on 12 July 1931, at Saint-Piât (Eure-et-Loir), that he had been matriculated at the École Normale Supérieure in 1951, and that prior to his election he had served private industry as an *"ingenieur conseil."*

While not much, it proved to be enough.

* * *

Not surprisingly, the institutions that school the sons of *la grande bourgeoisie,* the French ruling class, are referred to as the *grandes écoles.* Of these, three are known for disproportionate representation at the highest levels of government service; the Polytéchnique, the Ecole Nationale d'Administration, and the Ecole Normale Supérieure.

The Ecole Normale Supérieure was created by the Convention in 1794 as a school for higher studies for those entering the teaching profession. In 1847 it was transferred to the buildings it now occupies in the rue d'Ulm, between the Panthéon and the rue Gay-Lussac. It was Fredericks's first stop on the *route fonctionnaire,* that path that leads from privileged birth to stewardship of the nation's institutions.

Accepting with equanimity the frosty declaration of an elderly factotum in the office of the registrar that school records were privileged, Fredericks's face was nonetheless troubled as he apologetically explained that he was charged with a mission of a *certaine délicatesse.*

Queried, Fredericks explained that he was acting as the executor of his recently deceased mother's estate.

Condolences were expressed.

His mother, Fredericks explained, like himself, an ardent Francophile, had, during the year preceding her marriage and his birth, been a student at the Beaux Arts.

A nod of saddened congratulation.

During which period, Fredericks further explained, she had formed a sympathetic liaison with a young French student then matriculated at the École Normale Supérieure.

A gentle smile, at once discreet and worldly: a fatuous observation on Paris and youth.

Which, continued Fredericks, brought him to the melancholy task with which he was charged. There were papers, he explained; some personal letters, some official documents sealed and notarized 34 years past. These had been kept in his mother's private safe-deposit box; it was her testamentary wish that they be delivered, unopened and by Fredericks alone, to her springtime friend, of whom, *hélas,* Fredericks knew but the last name.

Did he mean...? Fredericks was asked.

With simple dignity Fredericks assured the elderly clerk that were he able to help him discharge this filial duty he would have the gratitude not only of his mother's executor but of, at least, his mother's son.

Clearly moved, the man straightened his back, brushed his *rosette,* finger-combed his mustache, and invited Fredericks into his office.

In a matter of such sensitivity, it was clearly important to foreclose, insofar as possible, any chance of error. To this end, Fredericks vouchsafed to the elderly clerk such meager information as was his. It was his understanding, for instance, that the student in question was of a mercantile family, whose seat was in the *pays* of the Beauce, near Chartres. And it was his further understanding that there had been a brother, elder, Fredericks thought, though perhaps younger, who was himself a *normalien.*

The fit was incontrovertible. There was indeed a Cassin—one Jean-Jacques—matriculated at that time, from a family (the clerk assured Fredericks) less happily described as mercantile than as dynastic in French industry, and, finally and conclusively, a brother, born (like Jean-Jacques) at Saint-Piât, who had preceded him at the ENS by four years. The entry, though spare, was eloquent to Fredericks:

Cassin, Yves: né le 8 Oct. 1925 á Saint-Piât (E&L): mat. 12 Sept. '49.

Fredericks thanked the elderly clerk with a heartfelt sincerity consonant with the solemnity of the occasion and took his leave.

Ah, Uncle Yves, thought Fredericks as he turned into the rue Gay-Lussac and joined the pedestrian traffic strolling toward the Luxembourg Gardens, what do you look like, you son of a bitch? What do you *do*?

The village of Saint-Piât lies in the quiet, wheat-growing country of the Beauce, an hour-and-a-half's pleasant drive from Paris. It is a small village, well west of the main road from Paris to Chartres. From its center one can see the roofs of perhaps a dozen houses, their faces hidden by the ubiquitous blind walls of the small French village, half a dozen shops, and three cafés.

Of the three, the Café des Sports is the most fortunately located. Facing onto the place, its back gives onto the Eure river, which bisects the town. Passing through its drab interior, with its dull zinc bar, its sleeping television set and "baby-foot" game, the fortunate traveler emerges onto a lovely old vine-covered wooden porch set out over the river. The waters move slowly by, tugging gently at the lily pads, and an old, unused mill, straddling the weir, smiles on the river with the equanimity of a contented old man watching his grandchildren at play.

It was there that Fredericks lunched. He was given a large plate of fresh *crudités*, country ham, and fresh bread, a lovely omelette with wood mushrooms, then cheese and fruit, all set with an unlabeled bottle of the sturdy and respectable *vin du pays*.

When the *patronne* brought him coffee, Fredericks complimented the luncheon and asked if he might make reference to her restaurant in an article that he was writing.

"Ah, you're a writer, then?" she said. "English?"

American, Fredericks confessed, and, yes, insofar as putting pen to paper made one such, he was a writer.

"A writer for tourists?" she asked, her eyes brightening. "Tourists never come here, you know. They go to see the Cathedral, eat swill in the town, and return to Paris the same day."

"A journalist, actually," Fredericks said, "with *The New York Times....*"

"*The New York Times!*" she exclaimed. "Louis, bring the *marc!*"

A man whom Fredericks presumed to be her husband emerged from the kitchen, a bottle dangling from his fist. He was red-eyed and unshaven, and the condition of his fingernails sharply compromised the pleasure Fredericks had recently taken in his lunch.

Glasses were filled: toasts drunk to wealthy tourists and *The New York Times*.

The article that he was writing, Fredericks explained, was not strictly for the tourist trade, but rather a survey of *"Les Familles Maîtresses de la Nouvelle France."* He had come to Saint-Piât, he continued, to visit the ancestral seat of the family Cassin, without reference to which any such survey would surely be incomplete.

"But, of course!" she exclaimed. "The Cassins! Pride and product of Saint-Piât...."

"They moved," her husband said, belching. "They got rich, and they moved to the capital."

"Pay no attention," she said sharply. "He is a drunkard and a fool. The house is just out of town on the D24, a handsome..."

"No Cassins there, though," the man said. "Soon as they got rich, poof!"

"They travel," she explained. "His mind is corroded with jealousy and drink. Pay no attention."

"Actually," Fredericks said, "I'd like very much to talk to someone who knew the family, particularly the last generation. Would there be schoolmates? A priest, perhaps?"

"A priest?" the man laughed, topping up the glasses. "What do the rich want with priests?"

"That's enough, you drunken windbag!" she snarled, and then her face suddenly brightened. "Madame Germaine! You should speak to Madame Germaine!"

"A senile old cunt," the man offered. "Save your time."

"Back to the kitchen!" she shouted. "A woman of great learning, who for many years was the tutor and governess of the Cassin family. Advanced in years, surely, but nonetheless the person to whom you should talk."

"I should like very much to speak with her," Fredericks said. "Do you think it would be possible?"

150

"And why not?" she said aggressively. "After all, an article in *The New York Times*...? Wait here, let me call her."

She disappeared into the café, taking the bottle of *marc* with her.

The landlord reached for the bottle before he noticed that it was gone. Fredericks pushed his glass across the table. "Before I married," the man said, wiping his mouth and placing the empty glass back in front of Fredericks, "I had plans. Plans, you know?"

Fredericks knew.

"I was to be a veterinarian," he sighed. "A good job. If not for the woman, I, too, would be in the capital today. I could have been someone big in poodles."

The woman returned, flushed with success.

"Madame Granvilliers will see you at three this afternoon," she announced proudly.

Having been given directions, Fredericks thanked them both and stood to leave.

"The Café des Sports," she said. "Lunch and dinner at reasonable prices on the banks of the Eure."

"There's money in poodles, you know," the man said.

The house of Madame Germaine Granvilliers, one of four in the rue du Général Leclerc, was being consumed by a wisteria vine. Rising from a trunk as thick as a man's waist, its tendrils shrouded the front porch and burrowed beneath the shingles above before disappearing over the low roof, headed, Fredericks assumed, for the back door in order to foreclose any possible escape.

The impressive antiquity of both house and vine, however, paled beside that of the figure who responded to Fredericks's tentative knock.

The shoes were black as were the stockings and severely cut suit. At the throat, which could not have been more than four feet from the floor, there sprouted a profusion of alençon lace, in which, like a desiccated crabapple and very nearly as bald, nestled the tiny head of his hostess.

Madame Granvilliers spoke without preamble.

"My namesake," she said, "Madame de Staël, spoke of the Americans as 'the future of the human race.' We must remember, however, that she also considered Joucourt and Narbonne to be moderates. Both judgments were premature: One, at least, erroneous. Won't you come in?"

The room into which Fredericks was led seemed more museum than sitting room, the repository of a lifetime's acquisitions. Three marquetry pieces—a desk, a highboy, and a chest of drawers—filled the near wall. Two antique lithographs, cherubs in the manner of Fragonard depicting Chastity and Prudence, hung above the desk. A low table supported a glass display case filled with *chinoiserie*. The far wall, shelved, held the heavy, black volumes of the 1905 Larousse; curtains of burgundy velvet stood guard against whatever light managed to penetrate the wisteria. The room smelled of old book and old lady, equally.

"Tea?" she asked. The table behind which she sat was carefully covered with a yellowed doily and held a freshly polished Regency tea service. Her eyes were bright with excitement.

"Please," Fredericks said, "if it's not too much trouble."

"Not at all," Madame Granvilliers assured him. "Marie!" she called.

A simpering young village girl, drafted, Fredericks assumed, for the occasion, entered with hot water.

"I must tell you," Madame Granvilliers said as the tea steeped, "that I consider my role in the later success of my students to be a peripheral one."

Fredericks demurred.

"No, no," she said. "I can teach them only to read and to write, to understand the history of their civilization and their race, and to discern and discharge the duties of their station. Beyond that, they must listen to their conscience and the voice of their God. Sugar?"

"Please," Fredericks said. "I understand, Madame Granvilliers, that you were the governess both of Jean-Jacques and Yves Cassin?"

"I hold fast to one rule, and one rule only, in the education of the aristocracy," the old lady continued, very nearly oblivious to Fredericks's presence. "It is this: *never allow them to read Rousseau.* A young mind so corrupted is easy prey to atheism, antimonarchism, *constitutionalism....*"

"Madame Granvilliers...." Fredericks began.

"Ask yourself," she continued firmly, "what has been the spawn of his immoral seed. Danton, Robespierre...."

"We would like," Fredericks said, "a picture to accompany our article...."

"...the Communards and sans-culottes...."

"...a picture," Fredericks continued, "which would include not only Jean-Jacques and Yves, but also the teacher from whom they received the foundation of learning on which their later lives were built."

"Saint-Just, Hébert, the Jacobin scum... picture?"

"A picture of you together with Jean-Jacques and Yves, Madame Granvilliers. Would you have such a picture that we might borrow?"

"I must tell you," the old lady said after a period of reflection, "that I consider my role in the later success of my students to be a peripheral one...."

Tea *chez* Madame Granvilliers proved lengthy: a life-long habit of pedagogy, stiffened by the single-gle-mindedness of senility, lends itself little to dialogue. At length, however, modesty overcome, reservations assuaged, Lamartine's handling of the Montagnards regretted, a picture suitable for *The New York Times* was selected from a shoebox brimming with memorabilia.

The picture had been taken while on summer holiday in Biarritz in 1935. Madame Granvilliers and her charges stood before a luxury automobile, in the *de rigueur* pose of that period. The younger child, clinging anxiously to the hand of his governess, Fredericks assumed to be Jean-Jacques.

The identity of his elder brother, however, formally dressed and facing the camera with a clear and unsmiling gaze, required no assumption at all on Fredericks's part, for through the dust and across the years the child who was father to the man "Laloux" regarded him, quite clearly.

FIFTEEN

FREDERICKS CALLED STUARTI from a café in the avenue du Maine. Responding, Stuarti said ungraciously that not only was there no Mademoiselle Cunégonde at the number that Fredericks had reached, but that, in the improbable event that there ever were, she would surely not wish to speak with an interlocutor so boorish as to call during the dinner hour.

Fredericks hung up chuckling, spent 15 minutes at the bar nursing a *demi*, then dialed the number of the pay telephone at La Palette, a café in the rue de Seine not 50 meters from Stuarti's apartment. The first time he tried the number it was busy; the second time Stuarti answered.

"Cassoulet," Stuarti said. "Excellent hot, an abomination cold. *Qu'est-ce que c'est* the fuck, *alors?*"

"Is that how you talk to all your customers, Mary? It's a wonder you stay in business," Fredericks said.

"A customer, are we? A paying customer? Quite different, dear boy. Won't you sit down?"

"You have some news for me, Mary?" Fredericks asked.

"What happened to the 'paying customer' part?" Stuarti said. "I *liked* that part, especially, the 'paying'...."

"Not to worry, Mary, virtue is its own reward. What've you got?"

"On our friend Laloux," Stuarti sniffed, "nothing. Burnham, however, is a different story."

"Go ahead."

"Thursday has become haircut day," Stuarti said. "Afterwards, he spends up to an hour and a half in the signal room. Also, Blaine knows him, at least to the point of looking *very* pained while denying it. What *I* think, dear boy, is that our friend Burnham is running an Illegal, probably French, and that the operation is independent of Paris station, which both explains why Blaine's nose is out of joint and suggests that the fish is a large one."

"Bravo, Mary," Fredericks said.

"There is, however, a point on which I am confused, dear boy. Perhaps you might enlighten me?"

"By all means," Fredericks said.

"Thursday last," Stuarti said, "I spent at Burnham's apartment...."

"What?" Fredericks said.

"He lives in the rue de l'Yvette. There's a little park opposite the building, ideal for taking the sun."

"What happened?" Fredericks asked.

"An experience as wounding to self-image as to sensibility," Stuarti said. "Why do women assume that old men long to dandle babies? I hadn't been in the park fifteen minutes before one was pressed on me. Loathsome. Thirty years of European encrustation notwithstanding, the little fucker immediately made me as an American. Peed right in my hand. Doing his little part for the Atlantic Alliance, one assumes. God, I detest the French!"

"Mary," Fredericks said.

"It occurred to me," Stuarti resumed, "that if he spends an hour and a half in the signal room, we may assume it likely that he does his own buttoning and unbuttoning. Since no one likes to run around a whole long time with a pocketful of rather compromising raw intelligence, it seems reasonable to assume equally that Thursday might also be shopping day."

"And...?" Fredericks said.

"He came out a little after nine, went somewhere on foot for a half-hour, and came back. The thing is, dear boy, that he had two sitters. On him like a blanket. And, interestingly enough, they did *not* look American. No black lace-up shoes, no Alumicron suits, no crew-cuts, not even *ties*. Can you think why an American case officer gets French protection while running a burn against a French target?"

"No idea, Mary," Fredericks said. "Who was it said, 'Where there's no paradox, there's no life'?"

"Let me put the question another way," Stuarti said after a censorious pause. "Who, precisely, is he being protected *from?*"

"Remember those papers I mentioned, Mary? The full set of custom French? I've got the particulars. I'd like them as soon as possible."

"It wouldn't be *you*, would it, dear boy?"

"Got a pencil?" Fredericks asked. "This is the 'paying customer' part." When Stuarti had arranged himself Fredericks began to provide the details. "Last name, *Cassin*, first name, *Yves*, born 8 October, 1925 at Saint-Piât, Eure et Loire...."

"Spell it for me," said Yves Cassin, shifting the telephone to his left shoulder and uncapping his pen.

"Just like it sounds," Burnham said, "last name

Stuarti, with a 'u,' first name Edward, spelled the English way."

"Go ahead," Cassin said.

"From what I'm told," said Burnham, "he's an old faggot, wears capes and lives on the Left Bank. Got himself on the payroll after the war as a contract occasional, and ever since then he's been getting the odd piece of change out of Paris station."

"Doing what?" Cassin asked.

"Mostly safe houses, as far as I can tell," Burnham said, "but apparently he did papers for the OSS types right after the war. Makes his living buying paintings for foreign clients. Rumor says that if he can't find what they want he's not above whacking it out himself."

"Ah," Cassin said, writing.

"He's also done a little talent spotting *chez* the left-handers in the *Quartier Latin*," Burnham continued. "Gets the kid in bed with him first, with us second."

"Shocking," Cassin said.

"Interesting, actually," Burnham said. "One of his enduring conquests—this is some twelve years ago—was a young Yugoslav student at the Sorbonne, name of Lazar Todorović. Kid went home, made good, became a big-wig journalist...."

"A nice source," Cassin said.

"Not anymore," Burnham said. "He was one of the ones that went into the bag when Fredericks's Novi Sad trip went bang. He's dead."

"As is, if I recall the file correctly, the UDBA double who tipped him in...?"

"Marićić," Burnham said. "There are people who think that it was Stuarti who told Fredericks where he could be found. He denies it, of course."

"Do you have an address?" Cassin asked.

"Number 1, rue Cardinale," Burnham said.

"I'll be in touch, Mr. Burnham."

The next Thursday again dawned sunny, and at 7:30 Stuarti sent his Moroccan houseboy Maddy (a nickname derived from Proust's biscuit; the merest taste of the boy, as it pleased Stuarti to explain, violently recalling first youth) to fetch the car.

Thirty years and more spent in a succession of delicate callings had honed, rather than blunted, the edge of Stuarti's tradecraft; he had not reached the quais before he was aware that he was being followed by two men in a blue Renault.

Making no effort at all to lose them, Stuarti drove along the Quai Anatole France as far as the Pont de la Concorde. Here he signaled and turned into the swarming morning traffic in the enormous place. By the time he reached the base of the Champs-Elyseés there was no longer any doubt; the blue Renault, in a violation of probability sufficient to foreclose the possibility of coincidence, was but two cars behind him.

The morning traffic ascending the great avenue was choked, each lane packed with slowly moving vehicles; from the place de la Concorde, the Arc de Triomphe was blurred and indistinct through the heavy diesel air.

Fearful of losing Stuarti in the traffic, the SDECE surveillance team was forced to keep the distance close. Approaching the first stoplight, Stuarti suddenly accelerated, then braked immediately and prematurely as the yellow light flashed. Flicking a glance in the rear-view mirror, Stuarti noticed with satisfaction that the maneuver had worked; the blue

Renault, with its two impassive passengers, was now directly behind him.

Moving to the next light, Stuarti eased into the far right lane, behind a No. 73 bus. To the rear, he could hear the blare of an angry horn as the blue Renault squeezed in behind him. He smiled, but he did not look back.

The traffic inched its way up the Champs-Elysées, now a single, inexorably moving mass.

Near the top of the avenue, there is, on the right, the entrance to a tunnel by-pass of the place de l'Étoile, for those who are continuing on toward Neuilly and wish to avoid the rush-hour chaos around the Arc de Triomphe. Immediately prior to its entrance, there is a stop for the No. 73 bus, a single hole left in an otherwise unbroken line of parked cars.

As the bus pulled out of its stopping place, Stuarti pulled quietly in, out of the traffic flow, and slipping the car into neutral, simply waited.

The men in the blue Renault hesitated behind him; once in front of him, they would be forced into the first choice, that between taking the by-pass or of entering the Etoile traffic, with its many possible exits.

The cacophony of horns and policemen's whistles began behind them. Stuarti sat quite quietly, praying that the operational brief of his new companions was limited to surveillance. The Renault, forced finally to move, passed Stuarti slowly, both men regarding him with an incuriosity that he found chilling.

Stuarti returned the inspection with a flirtatious, camping smile, and as they passed he jerked his car into the traffic directly behind them.

At the entrance to the by-pass, the SDECE car

attempted to straddle both lanes, in the hope that Stuarti would commit himself. Squarely behind them, Stuarti led the chorus of protesting horns.

Forced to decision, the blue Renault finally swung left, heading on toward the Etoile. Stuarti, with a gentle wave, slipped into the by-pass and was gone.

Twenty minutes later, his car parked in a garage nearby, he was unfolding the previous day's edition of *Le Monde* in the small garden in the rue de l'Yvette, his boutonniere bright in the morning sun, his eyes fixed on Burnham's building.

Stuarti, elegant in a muted stripe, regarded Fredericks with distaste across their aperitifs. "Wherever did you get that suit, dear boy? You look like something rural dressed for church."

"At the *Marché aux Puces*," Fredericks smiled, "a hundred and fifty francs. Like it?"

Stuarti shuddered.

"After all, Mary," Fredericks said, "I'm supposed to be Belgian."

"That's it," Stuarti said. "Just the word I was looking for. That suit is positively Belgian. Odious."

"Next time I'll dress up," Fredericks said.

"Next time," Stuarti said slowly, "may be a tenuous proposition. I was followed this morning when I left my apartment."

Fredericks's eyes held Stuarti's for a moment in a hard, flat stare, shifted briefly to the door, returned.

"What?" he asked quietly.

"*Du calme,* dear boy," Stuarti said. "I dumped them at the Etoile. Two men in suits, very much like yours, actually, driving a blue Renault. Paris plates."

"It could be something else, Mary."

"It could be a *hundred* something elses," Stuarti agreed, "but it's not. The vast majority of my something elses are nice, straightforward felonies. Lock me up, I might think it's a something else—tail me, I think it's you. My name's bound to be in your file."

"Quite sure you lost them, are you?" Fredericks asked.

"Absolutely, dear boy. I was in the little park opposite Burnham's at eight forty-five."

"What happened there?"

"A repeat performance," Stuarti said with satisfaction. "Out the front door on foot at nine fifteen, goes off somewhere with his sitters. They come back twenty minutes later, he comes back at ten or so. He was still upstairs when I left to come here. Dirty Thursday, dear boy, count on it."

"Upstairs?"

Stuarti smiled. "Four-B. When he went for his little walk I strolled inside, took a look at the mailboxes. There's also an ongoing construction project, although it currently seems to be on hold, on the lot adjacent to the rear of his building. It should be possible to get a wire on in a pinch, were one so inclined."

The waiter came to take their orders. Reassured that the *rouille* was made fresh daily, and that Fredericks was paying, Stuarti ordered the *soupe de poissons* and *poulet à l'estragon*. Fredericks asked for a rare steak and a green salad.

"You have papers for me, Mary?" Fredericks asked.

"Everything but a passport. For that, I need a

photograph first. For the driver's license, you just staple on a photo yourself."

Stuarti removed a cheap, leather wallet, used, from his suit coat and handed it to Fredericks.

"The wallet is free, dear boy," he said, emphasizing the word "wallet."

"And the rest?" Fredericks asked, pocketing the wallet.

"As near cost price as I can force myself to come, dear boy. Let's say six thousand French."

"There's ten thousand in an envelope in the newspaper," Fredericks said, not looking at the folded *Le Figaro* on the table between them. "What were your plans for the afternoon?"

"Well," Stuarti was reflecting, "I *could* go home, take a nice nap like the other seniors. In view of the fact, however, that I would probably be arrested before I got the car stopped and hauled off somewhere to have my toenails torn out until I told them your blood type, I would be loath to do so."

"Understandable," Fredericks said.

"Actually, I was thinking of taking a wee vacation. Thought I might visit my friend Roland in Taormina for a few weeks. There's a flight this afternoon at 4:45. Perhaps I'll call home after lunch—I assume that they've got a loop on by now—and say that I won't be home till six or so. With a little luck, I should be drinking a cassis on the beach before they've even got the alligator clips fastened to Maddy's dick."

"Good idea, Mary," Fredericks said. "You could use a little sun. Got enough money?"

"Unless you've put Monopoly money in the envelope, dear boy, I think I should be fine for at least a month, thank you."

"Figure three weeks, tops," Fredericks said. "Either way, you'll be all right by then."

"I see," Stuarti said after a long pause. "You're quite sure you don't need me here, then?"

"Actually, Mary, I could use one more thing."

"Such as?"

"I could use the name of this season's friendly KGB talent-spotter," Fredericks said, "preferably a legal. I'll take a GRU man in a pinch, but the KGB always seems to have more money."

There was an even longer pause before Stuarti spoke. "Frankly, dear boy, I don't think that you'd like it there. Dull food, dowdy clothes, horrid climate, depressing police presence...."

"Get stuffed," Fredericks said crisply. "Have you got a name?"

"Why, yes," Stuarti's face relaxed. "At a senior level one might consider one Vyacheslav Petkov. He's nominally a consular trade official, with an office in the consulate in the rue de Grenelle. He also keeps an office in the Banque Commerciale de l'Europe du Nord, which is Soviet-owned, in the avenue Raymond Poincaré. Lives his cover quite well, apparently, but he's definitely a hood."

"Thank you, Mary," Fredericks said.

They said goodby on the sidewalk outside the restaurant. The sun had faded; the afternoon was gull gray and chill.

Slightly in wine, Stuarti embraced Fredericks farewell. When he did so, his hand encountered the gun beneath the jacket of Fredericks's cheap suit.

"Dear boy," he said, his arms dropping to his sides and his face troubled. "Going to shoot someone, are we?"

"Yes," Fredericks said.

Stuarti regarded Fredericks's expressionless face for a long moment before he spoke, his voice empty of banter.

"I am sufficiently your senior to permit myself a liberty. Noah, it's this—don't forget the name of the cause in which you act. It can be absolutely anything—To Foster Truth, Honor, and the American Way, To Make the World Safe for Democracy, To Protect the Sacred Whoopee from the Ever-Encroaching Ding-Dong—but believe me, the fiction is a necessary one. You've been wronged, I grant it, but the merely *tu quoque* argument of revenge is insufficient, and will sicken you. Don't..."

Here Stuarti hesitated.

"Don't...?" Fredericks said softly.

"Don't learn to love it, dear boy."

"Goodby, Mary," Fredericks said.

SIXTEEN

THE BRANCH BANK of Crédit Lyonnais that Fredericks had used for his personal banking was in the rue Saint-Croix de la Bretonnerie in the fourth arrondissement. There, for the past three years, he had maintained a checking account, a small thrift account to avoid service charges, and a safety-deposit box.

There also, alas, his account had been flagged and his safety deposit box confiscated; a car with two impassive passengers was parked daily across the street, and the desk in accounting formerly occupied by Madame Moreau had been appropriated by a new employee, a taciturn man who even on the warmest of spring days maintained his jacket.

Fredericks, understandably, would not have come within ten blocks.

There was, however, another bank, a branch office of Société Générale in the seventeenth arrondissement, where Fredericks kept another safety-deposit box, for which he paid cash, annually. He maintained there neither savings nor checking account, and the billing records for safety-deposit boxes are kept by number.

Fredericks had to take the risk.

At 10:00 on this bright May morning, Fredericks had coffee in a café opposite the bank. He sat near the windows, abstractedly watching the traffic. He had two cups.

From 10:30 till 11:00, an ambitious young platform officer of the bank detailed to an appreciative Fredericks, as they sat at his desk, the intricacies of mortgage financing, and when, pursuant to a discussion of possible collateral, Fredericks expressed a wish to make reference to certain papers in his safety-deposit box, the young loan officer saved them both time by obtaining the box with Fredericks's key, returning with it, and showing Fredericks to a private carel.

At 11:20, gratitude expressed and cards exchanged, Fredericks left the bank. In his jacket pocket were three containers of film. His shirt, beneath the jacket, was sodden with sweat.

The day, of course, was unseasonably warm.

When working at his office in the avenue Raymond Poincaré, Consular Officer Vyacheslav Petkov regularly parked his car in the enormous two-tiered parking garage beneath the avenue Foch.

Eight blocks in length, the parking garage Foch, like many modern urban addenda, was engineered more for automobiles than for their merely organic adjuncts. A sign at each entranceway advises drivers to lower their radio antennae before entering, for the ceilings are only six feet high. Ill-lit and poorly ventilated, the atmosphere is claustrophobic.

As he locked his car and hurried toward the exit some hundred yards distant, Vyacheslav Petkov was badly startled when a large, stooped figure emerged, with disquieting suddenness, from between two cars and addressed him by name.

"Gospodin Petkov?" Fredericks said quietly.

Sweat broke instantly on Petkov's brow. Twenty years of service with the KGB does not leave one without enemies. The figure in front of him was only silhouetted by the light behind, but Petkov, though at fifty-one still a sturdily built man, realized sickly as he saw the shoulders and hands that if he reached for his pocket his arm would be broken before his fingers touched the fabric; if he called out, it could as easily be his neck.

"Who are you?" Petkov said in excellent French, his voice admirably contained.

The figure before him said nothing, regarding him with a relaxed and chilling silence.

"Please," Petkov mustered an indignant tone, "what is it that you wish?" His voice, this time, was somewhat less reliable.

"Listen carefully, Mr. Petkov." The fact that Fredericks's voice was soft did nothing to diminish its authority.

"You're American," Petkov said. "American or English."

"That's not listening." Fredericks rocked forward onto the balls of his feet. "That's talking."

Petkov nodded, very careful not to speak.

"Who I am," Fredericks said in English, "is of no importance. What I have to say may be. I am a literary agent, Gospodin Petkov. I represent a free-lance journalist who wishes to know what the market, if you'll pardon the formulation, in the Soviet Union might be for certain essays of a highly specialized nature."

"I have nothing to do with literature," Petkov said. "I am a consular trade official. Perhaps..."

"And I'm the fucking tooth fairy," Fredericks said. "Shut your goddamned mouth."

Petkov closed his mouth.

"My client," Fredericks said, "is willing to provide samples before discussing terms."

Fredericks's hand went to his pocket and iron bands tightened around Petkov's chest. When the hand was withdrawn, however, there were only three film containers in the broad, flat palm.

"These essays are previously unpublished," Fredericks said. "They derive from ongoing work at the Lincoln Laboratory of the Massachusetts Institute of Technology."

Fredericks indicated the canister nearest to Petkov with his thumb.

"Simulation of Exo-Atmospheric Attack: Working Paper No. 1: Ellipsoidal Chaff-Cloud Model."

Petkov took it.

"Simulation of Exo-Atmospheric Attack: Working Paper No. 2: A Logical Structure for the Restart Capability. Take it."

Petkov took it.

"Simulation of Exo-Atmospheric Attack: Working Paper No. 3: Variable Viewing Plane: A Mathematical Camera."

Petkov took it.

Petkov held the three canisters in his hand. "The subjects are, indeed, highly specialized," he began. "I shall have to bring them to the attention of our consular scientific attaché...."

"No," Fredericks said. "You have to get them into the diplomatic bag as soon as possible. You have no local authority to disburse the funds required for further material. I will telephone you at the consulate one week from today, in the morning. I will identify myself as Monsieur Léon. Should you wish to commission additional...'articles' ...we will arrange a meeting. If not, you will not be contacted again. Do you understand?"

"I must know more," Petkov said, shaking his head. "For instance, your client...."

"Do you understand?"

"Yes," Petkov said.

"Now walk to your office," Fredericks said. "Walk slowly. If you look around or attempt to follow me, I'll kill you."

Petkov began walking, stiffly. Spiders of sweat tickled his back. Fear nauseated him. Servant of a system built on a mountain of corpses, he was an adept at distinguishing real killers from false.

Fredericks entered the Métro at the station Argentine.

The materials that he had given Petkov were the laborious product of an abandoned disinformation project on which he had worked four years prior. It would take far longer than a week to prove them false; the access that they indicated insured that Petkov would nonetheless be ordered to return for a second bite.

Entering the first-class carriage, Fredericks was aware of an odd sense of buoyancy, of that exhilaration that sometimes and inappropriately accompanies fever. As the train began to gather speed, Fredericks's lips drew slowly back from his teeth in what for all the world he thought a smile, and his thick hands began to flex unconsciously, again and again.

Soon after his election to the National Assembly, it became evident, as Jean-Jacques Cassin explained to his wife, that the exigencies of his office—almost as much as its concomitant perquisites—required the maintenance of an apartment in Paris.

To this end he leased an elegant and tax-deductible *pied-à-terre* in the rue Théodule-Ribot in the seventeenth arrondissement, to which he referred, on his increasingly infrequent visits to the large private house in Le Pecq that was home to Madame Cassin and the small Cassins three, as his *bureau privé* ("private office" seeming a more compelling formulation in the context of such discussions than "love nest").

Once, alas, in a rare access of boldness, Madame Cassin had driven the twenty minutes from Le Pacq to surprise her husband of an evening.

Although, miraculously, Jean-Jacques had been alone, the visit had not been a success.

A practical woman, Madame Cassin had found the absence of a desk and the presence of a double bed suspect in the appointment of a *bureau privé:* The discovery of a pessary in the cabinet beneath the sink, loftily dismissed by Jean-Jacques as belonging either to a previous tenant or to the cleaning woman, and of Rodinger Brüt in the refrigerator had turned suspicion to acrimony.

Harsh words were exchanged; Madame Cassin inquiring prettily into the usefulness of such accoutrements to "an asshole unable to get it up with a jack," Monsieur Cassin responding that while checking the pillow slips for lipstick might be expected from a fishwife, rooting in the sheets for foreign pubic hairs was an act he would heretofore have considered beneath the dignity of even the "unnatural sow" whom it was his misfortune to call helpmate.

Though it was not an incident to which they frequently referred, resentment lingered.

Thus when at 6:30 in the evening an anxious functionary from the Chamber of Deputies, whose name she did not bother to note, telephoned their home to report that important papers had arrived for immediate transmittal to her husband, Madame Cassin vouchsafed, with alacrity and against standing orders to the contrary, not only the address of Jean-Jacques' *pied-à-terre*, but the fervent wish that the papers might keep him up all night.

Hanging up, she smiled with satisfaction, filled her glass with that mother's helper known as *vin gris*, and rejoined the children and the governess for the evening's episode of *Un, rue Sésame*.

Fredericks, too, was smiling as he left the phone booth, folded the address into his pocket, and hailed a cab.

The building in the rue Théodule-Ribot was an elegant five-story *hôtel particulier* surrounding a gardened courtyard. The heraldic salamander of François I in the masonry above the entranceway laid subtle (and factitious) claim to an ancestry anchored in Valois rule; in fact, the structure dated from the early nineteenth century.

From the street Fredericks could see the light of the concierge's small booth to the left of the entranceway. Beyond, a staircase of Empire/Tara dimensions, carpeted in red plush, swept pretentiously from a lobby of marble and gilt to the second floor and the apartments above.

Fredericks identified himself to the concierge as calling on behalf of "Maître Bichet of Saint-Lô." After a conversation on the house telephone in which he was obliged to repeat himself three times and apologize twice, Fredericks was directed by the concierge to the staircase and the *deuxième à gauche*.

Jean-Jacques Cassin, *normalien* and *Député*, was waiting for Fredericks in the hallway outside the apartment. He no longer wore his suit coat, but the trousers and vest were expensively tailored, the tie a Hermès. His round head was slightly too large for his body, and his features, perhaps because of the petulance of the mouth, belied his age. His expression was one of practiced and haughty displeasure.

He waited imperially for Fredericks to approach before he spoke.

"Who are you?" Jean-Jacques asked icily. "And what could you possibly mean by disturbing me here?"

("The key to a successful burn," Richardson had taught, "lies in the management of the mark's pride. It's pride that allows hatred, and hatred that can stiffen the back. Break the pride, and you've got the mark. It is, gentlemen, a bully's game. Be loathsome, wall-slamming, rude. Your object is to make the mark wish for nothing so much as your disappearance from his life.")

Fredericks regarded him from head to toe before he spoke. When he did so, it was without that deference to which Jean-Jacques was so clearly accustomed.

"Jesus," Fredericks said, smiling, "I'll bet they called you Pumpkin-Head when you were a kid."

Jean-Jacques Cassin's mouth sagged open.

"Close your mouth, Pumpkie," Fredericks said, "and listen carefully. Your brother is peddling his ass to the highest bidders and covering his with yours. Your little land fiddle in Saint-Lô—Bichet, Meillant, the cut-out note held by Cabinet Lalande, the whole works—is swelling up like a week-dead dog in the August sun, and when it goes bang you're going to have shit stuck all *over* you. Let's talk."

"Who are you?" Cassin asked again, but this time his voice was a whisper, his face ashen.

"Get rid of the broad," Fredericks said.

Alone in the apartment with Fredericks, his companion dismissed, the door safely closed behind them and a tumbler very nearly full of whisky in his hand, Jean-Jacques Cassin had sufficiently recovered his composure to repeat his question to Fredericks.

"It makes no difference who I am." Fredericks helped himself to the drink that Jean-Jacques had forgotten to offer.

"You're American," Jean-Jacques said, accusingly.

"Christ, why does everyone *say* that?" Fredericks asked. "Is it my r's? Here, listen. *Rue. Roi. Rouge.* How's that?"

"You're a CIA agent," Cassin said.

Fredericks walked over to Cassin's desk and picked up a silver-framed photograph of three small children in Sunday clothes.

"Yours?" Fredericks asked.

"Yes."

"Now what are you doing wasting your time with hookers when you've got three nice kids like these at home?" Fredericks asked.

"My life as a man and my life as a father are kept entirely separate," Cassin said stiffly.

"Right," Fredericks agreed cordially, "wouldn't do to fuck the kids, I guess."

"I'll thank you to leave my personal life out of this," Cassin said, coloring.

Fredericks replaced the photo on the desk and turned to Cassin, slowly.

"Ah, of course, your 'personal life'," he said. "I

know just how you feel. Had one myself a few weeks ago."

"And further," Cassin, who was not a good listener, said, "I'll thank you..."

"No, you won't, my friend," Fredericks said, "what you'll do is shut your fucking mouth and listen. And pay attention, too, because there's going to be a quiz, understand?"

While an otiose prig, Jean-Jacques Cassin was not a fool.

He sat down and listened.

Fredericks began bluntly.

"Sometime in the last six months," he said, "I think that your brother whacked out some sort of deal to provide—maybe give, probably sell—intelligence to the Americans."

"The Americans?" Jean-Jacques was incredulous.

"At *least* the Americans," said Fredericks. "For all I know, the bastard has a client list that reads like the Security Council roster."

"Why are you telling me this?" Jean-Jacques moaned. "I..."

"Be quiet," Fredericks said. "Now your brother is a careful man, and I think that we may assume that there would have to be certain safeguards built into such a deal before he would even consider it. First, there would have to be a cover adequate to sustain his servicing by a case officer. Second, he would have to have a fall-back position for insurance against any unforeseen shit hitting the fan. Your election, coupled with your little land fiddle in Saint-Lô, provided both."

"The bastard!" Jean-Jacques dramatically exclaimed. "I offer him a participation in the syndication, and he rewards me with treachery!"

"Bullshit. You wanted him in as additional protection against any undue curiosity on the part of the *Fisc*. He smelled a rat, declined politely, and went rat hunting. You tried to use him, he *did* use you. That's all."

Cassin sniffed and said nothing, privately celebrating, Fredericks assumed, the strength of the French family unit.

"So," Fredericks continued, "your brother points the Americans in your direction. They drop in an expendable agent to take a look, who promptly walks into the set-up with his eyes wide shut. With his arrest, there exists a fully documented run by a fully documented American agent at a French politician. The sort of problem, in short, that would necessitate consultation, at the least, between your brother and his American counterpart. Handy, those meetings. Now all he needs is insurance."

Cassin's eyes flickered away from Fredericks's face and rested briefly on his crooked and discolored little finger before returning.

"Of course," Fredericks continued, "you wear two hats. You are not only Jean-Jacques Cassin, RPR Deputy from the Yvelines, you are also Jean-Jacques Cassin, brother of a prominent colonel in the SDECE. It is this fact that provides your brother with his insurance. In the course of the interrogation following his arrest, the expendable American agent was kind enough to volunteer the fact that you were intended to be merely the tool with which to compromise a highly placed brother. As that brother might point out, should the necessity arise, *you don't try to blackmail someone you already have in your pocket.* Thanks to you, he's both covered *and* insured. Of course, *you're* a little naked, but then, that's not really his problem."

Cassin's high forehead was beaded with sweat, and the shirt beneath his arms was sodden. He compulsively turned a gold signet ring on his little finger with his thumb.

"Who else knows?" he finally asked, his voice strained.

"About your brother?"

"About the land syndication in Saint-Lô." Jean-Jacques did not meet Fredericks's eyes.

"Whoever else he's sold you to, I guess," Fredericks said.

"Merde, alors!" Jean-Jacques said.

"It *is* awkward," Fredericks agreed, refreshing his drink from the decanter on the table between them.

"Who *are* you?" Jean-Jacques blurted furiously. "What do you want?"

"To help you. Nothing more," Fredericks said. "Think of me as a family friend."

"How?" Cassin asked. "And how much?"

"Get a pencil, Pumpkie," Fredericks said.

"Where do you do your principal banking?" Fredericks asked.

"Crédit Lyonnais, thirty-seven place Vendôme."

"Fine. And what's the current assessed value of the syndicate's holdings in Saint-Lô?"

"Right now we carry it as a paper liability of three million eight hundred thousand new francs," Cassin said, "about eight hundred thousand dollars."

"Which means," Fredericks said, "if you go to the bank and show them *both* notes, they're going to see a cash value of at *least* two hundred thousand dollars, right?"

"Oh, Christ," Cassin moaned.

"Don't whine, Pumpkie," Fredericks said. "This isn't even gonna hurt. Now here's what you do. First, go to your nice friends at Crédit Lyonnais, and arrange the maximum loan possible against the Saint-Lô property as collateral. Tell them, also, that there will be a cosignatory to the note, whose name you'll provide at the closing."

Cassin looked up sharply.

"Second," Fredericks continued, "arrange for the note currently held in trust for you at Cabinet Lalande to be converted to joint-tenancy."

"Who's to be the joint tenant?" Cassin asked.

"Same as the cosignatory on the loan. Your loving brother."

"I can't," Cassin said, sagging. "He could ruin me."

Fredericks reached across the table and lifted Cassin's chin with his finger. "He's not the only one, my friend. But if you think you've really got a choice, I'll leave now and see if I can't get the letters into the late post."

"Oh, God!" Cassin moaned, bowing his head and running his hands through his thinning hair. He began to write.

In addition to the normal office console on Yves Cassin's desk, there were two black telephones. A typed message, bordered in red and taped to the receiver of each, identified them as active operational lines, and gave instructions for the operation of the tape recorder that sat between them, attached to both.

Shortly after three o'clock on the afternoon of May 20, the telephone to the left of the tape recorder rang stridently. It had not done so since its installation three weeks earlier, and its sudden sound startled Cassin badly. He lifted the receiver from its cradle before it could ring a second time and held it for a moment in his hand, staring. Despite the typed instructions, he did not activate the tape recorder. Finally, he breathed deeply, swallowed, and lifted the receiver cautiously to his ear.

"Hello?" he said.

"Colonel Laloux, please," Winthrop Burnham said.

"Speaking."

"You recognize the voice?" Burnham asked.

"Yes. What is it?"

"I have some good news...." Burnham began.

"What!" Cassin whispered furiously. "This line is only for use in *cas d'urgence!*"

"Well, it's *urgent* good news. I received a letter today from our friend. He's in New York."

Cassin noticed that the hand holding the receiver was white at the knuckles. He relaxed his grip, blotted his upper lip on the cuff of his shirt, and breathed deeply.

"What did he want?" he asked.

"Yes, I think it's just what we want," Fredericks said to the rental agent, looking around the elegantly furnished apartment in the rue Murillo that overlooked the parc Monceau. "Quiet, of course, is a consideration. We will be lodging our most important buyers here during the period of the *salons* and would not wish them to be disturbed either by street noise or noise from the adjacent apartments."

"Please, Monsieur." The rental agent was clearly injured at even the suggestion of such a possibility. "This building is of the *most* modern construction. The windows, as you can see, are all double-glazed. The walls are expressly insulated against noise. I assure you, the Battle of Ulm could be refought in the apartment next door and it would not awaken your dog."

Fredericks smiled, pleased (perhaps) by the man's trope, or (perhaps) by something else.

"Of course," the rental agent raised his finger in mock severity, "dogs are not permitted."

"Of course." Fredericks was smiling still.

"Fifteen thousand dollars?" Yves Cassin asked.

"It was the retainer and guarantee we agreed on for his little investigation," Burnham said. "He said that the check had been confiscated with his other papers and asked for reimbursement."

"That's it? No recriminations? No threats? He must know that he was set up."

"Hold on," Burnham said. "I've got it here.... 'I trust that I may depend on your honor in this regard, as you may depend on my continued discretion....' Sincerely, et cetera. I suppose that could be considered a threat."

"You pay him, he keeps his mouth shut. That sort of thing?" There was skepticism in Cassin's voice.

"I suppose so," Burnham said. "As if he hadn't volunteered my name first thing out of the blocks, the bastard."

"Can you hold the phone for a moment?" Cassin asked. "I'd like to check something in the files."

"Certainly," Burnham said.

"But most certainly," the rental agent said. "Linens, towels, whatever you wish."

"Fine," Fredericks said. "We'll also want to have the current locks changed, and our own installed."

"But of course. Such expenses, you understand, are the responsibility of the tenant."

"Naturally," Fredericks said.

Returning to the telephone with a typed list in his hand, Yves Cassin said, "No."

"No, what?"

"The check wasn't among the papers confiscated."

"What do you mean?" Burnham asked.

"What do you mean, 'What do you mean?' The...check...wasn't...among..."

"No, no." Burnham clung stubbornly to his agreeable vision of Fredericks in New York. "I mean, so what? Maybe he lost it. It hasn't been cashed, I checked."

"Perhaps," Cassin's voice was devoid of encouragement. "If so, it's not the only thing that's gotten lost lately."

"What do you mean?" Burnham asked before he could help himself.

"You'll recall our elderly homosexual friend?" Cassin said.

"Yes."

"I put a surveillance team on him a week ago today. Which he promptly made and lost, in spite of the fact that the *vieux con* can't even walk. He was dressed in a suit. No valise, no overcoat, no

186

toothbrush, nothing at all. And he's *gone*. The houseboy, a Moroccan illegal, says he doesn't have the slightest idea where, and I think we can believe him. All we know is that he was feeling sufficiently nervous about something to run like hell the instant he felt even a hint of hot breath on his neck."

"He's a crook," Burnham said. "If I'd done even *half* the stuff he's done, surveillance would make *me* nervous, too."

"I don't think so," Cassin said. "He's a professional, and what he does is difficult to prosecute, even if it gets to court. Somebody squawks about a painting, all he has to do is get huffy, take it back, and look for another slicker."

"Another *what*?"

"Someone else to buy the painting," Cassin said shortly.

"'Sucker'," Burnham said. "That's 'sucker'."

"Perhaps," Cassin said icily, after an extended pause, "our *pédé* friend is less nervous about past indiscretions than he is about on-going ones."

"Whatever," Burnham said impatiently. "We still can't tie him to Fredericks in any way."

"Oh, the houseboy did that," Cassin said with satisfaction, "picked his picture right out."

When Burnham spoke again, his voice was leaden.

"Shit."

"A la prochaine fois," Cassin said, hanging up.

"There is one other matter." The rental agent's pen was poised above the papers ranged before him on the escritoire. "I am sure you will understand."

"Please," Fredericks said.

"Our apartments are normally let on an annual basis," he said. "Thus, when the term is as short as you desire, we are obliged to ask for an incremental monthly sum to cover the period between rentals."

"Certainly," Fredericks said. "How much?"

"However," the dapper little man continued rapidly, not quite meeting Fredericks's eyes, "it is possible, through my influence with the owners, that such an increment could be reduced considerably were it to be paid in cash."

"Which you could convey to the owners?" Fredericks asked.

"At your service," the rental agent said. "I am sure they would accept one thousand francs."

"Excellent." Fredericks clapped him on the shoulder. "After all, it's the government that's paying."

"A pleasure to do business with Monsieur." The rental agent turned again with relief to his papers. "And the name of the lessee?"

"Cassin." Fredericks removed a battered leather wallet from his suit coat. "C-a-s-s-i-n. First name, Yves."

The letterhead of the corporate stationery of Schweitzer Eigentums Bank, A.G. indicates, reassuringly, that its head office is located in Zurich's Paradplatz and that it maintains representative offices in London, Paris, Amsterdam, Bahrain, Nassau, and Panama City.

Which is indeed the case.

The bank's corporate brochure, appropriately sober and expensively printed, describes its activities as concentrated in the areas of wholesale commercial banking, fiduciary services, money and securities markets, and corporate financial services.

This description, alas, is less than accurate.

Schweitzer Eigentums Bank, A.G. exists solely to aid those depositors, of whatever nationality, who consider their participation in their nation's various Internal Revenue programs to be disproportionate and who are willing to pay the bank's not inconsiderable fees for its aid in reducing such participation.

The services that it offers are two: the effecting of discreet cash transfers in such a manner that the resultant paper trail is, at best, nonexistent, and, at worst, incomprehensible; and the location of credible paper losses to offset the deposits of its customers.

They will not give you a toaster.

But then, Fredericks did not want a toaster.

What he wished, as he explained to Herr Dr. Walter Leverkühn in the Dr.'s private office overlooking the rue de Richelieu and the Bourse, was simply to open a private, numbered account in the bank's Zurich office.

"You understand," said Dr. Leverkühn, a featureless technocrat gray in every regard beyond his years, "that French banking laws require extensive registration information should you wish to make any transactions through this office. The type of account you wish cannot be used domestically, not even for an initial deposit or transfer."

"I understand perfectly," Fredericks said. "All transactions will be made through the Zurich office."

"There is a fee for the establishment of such an account of five hundred francs Swiss," Dr. Leverkühn said.

"Naturally," Fredericks said.

As Fredericks removed the leather wallet from his suit-coat, Dr. Leverkühn withdrew the necessary forms from his desk drawer and began to write.

"This, then," Dr. Leverkühn said, passing a slip of paper across the desk to Fredericks, "is the number of your account. Your transactions in the Zurich office will be handled by a Dr. Joseph Baer. The identifying name that you will give to Dr. Baer for such transactions will be Monsieur Léon, L-e-o-n. Is that correct?"

"Perfectly." Fredericks rose and offered his hand. "Thank you for your help, Dr. Leverkühn."

"A pleasure to be of service, Monsieur Cassin." The banker, shaking Fredericks's hand, showed him to the door, and forgot him forever.

SEVENTEEN

Having MOVED THAT morning to a small hotel in the rue Pergolése in the sixteenth, Fredericks enjoyed a late breakfast on the terrace of a café on the avenue de la Grande Armée. He ate fresh bread with *rillettes du porc,* drank a *ballon* of the season's Beaujolais, and, in the warmth, lingered over his coffee.

The day was brilliant, a summer clarity in the light deepening the shadows of the leaves on the pavement and sharpening the vivid colors of the posters that plastered a nearby kiosk, calling the attention of passersby to affairs of sexual scandal, violent death, and *la mode d'été.*

At 10:45, he settled his bill and obtained a *jeton* for the public telephone.

As he stood in the *cabine,* a sudden and unanticipated wave of longing for the sound of Danielle's voice washed over him, a desire as focused and elemental as hunger or thirst.

With an iron effort of will he put the need from him, dialing, instead, a number with a Trocadéro exchange.

Vyacheslav Petkov answered before it rang a second time.

"Bonjour," Fredericks said. "Monsieur Léon here. I believe you have a decision for me?"

"Monsieur Léon!" Petkov said warmly. "I'm very pleased you called. Pleased, also, to tell you that your client's articles are being read with the greatest interest. Although, naturally, the formal authorization of funds to commission further such articles cannot be obtained in a week, I am confident that..."

"Stop it," Fredericks said. "It's yes or no, and now."

"Yes," Petkov said.

"Fine," Fredericks said. "Be in the Tuileries, at the octagonal basin between the Jeu de Paume and the Orangerie, in thirty minutes. You'll be contacted there. Come alone."

"Monsieur Léon!" Petkov's voice was strained. "Please! All right! I agree! But another man, one only, must come with me. About this, believe me, I can do nothing."

"I believe you," Fredericks said after a pause. "They don't even trust you, do they, you poor bastard? You've got thirty minutes. I'd take a cab."

The phone went dead in Petkov's hand.

The brilliant weather had thronged the Tuileries with Parisians. Around the octagonal basin old ladies and nursemaids took the sun, their faces upturned and slightly stunned. Children shouted and ran on the warm gravel; some sailed toy boats on the basin, launching them with the prevailing breeze, then racing breathlessly to await them on the other side. Clouds of luminescent white scudded across the sky.

Even with the crowds, it was not difficult for Fredericks to distinguish Petkov and his companion as he approached from the Terrace des Feuillants. They sat stiffly on green metal chairs next to the basin. Both wore suits. Petkov held a black briefcase on his lap. His companion, young, thick, with short blond hair, held a loaf of bread from which he occasionally tore chunks to throw to the fish. He did not, however, look like a fish lover. He looked like a cop.

Petkov started violently when Fredericks's hand touched his shoulder.

"Don't get up," Fredericks said. "Who's your friend?"

"Monsieur Léon," Petkov said, "may I present Monsieur Arvid Yeremenko. Monsieur Yeremenko is a consular colleague, recently arrived from Moscow, also involved in matters of international trade."

"Sure," Fredericks said.

"Monsieur Yeremenko was most interested in the articles written by your client," Petkov continued bravely.

Fredericks regarded Yeremenko. His lashless eyes were very nearly without color. His head was smaller than his neck. He returned Fredericks's inspection coldly.

"Is that right, Monsieur Yeremenko?" Fredericks asked pleasantly.

"Yes." Yeremenko was unblinking.

"What's an ellipsoidal chaff-cloud?" Fredericks asked.

Yeremenko continued to regard Fredericks for a moment, then slowly tore a piece of bread from the loaf he was holding. He flipped the bread into the water and an enormous carp, obscenely variegated in reds and whites, appeared and took it with a soft popping sound. With thick fingers, bitten to the cuticle and caked with grime, he tore another chunk from the loaf and put it into his mouth. As he began to chew he smiled at Fredericks. He said nothing.

"Monsieur Yeremenko is a metallurgist," Petkov said, smiling painfully.

"Is that right?" Fredericks was still staring at Yeremenko. "One of Botvinnik's best tournaments was in a Trade Union Spartakiad. He played for the Chemists, against the Metallurgists. You guys must have a good time, all those clubs. Chemists versus Metallurgists, Zeks versus The New Class...."

Yeremenko threw in two more pieces of bread. Almost instantly the water began to churn.

"Please," Petkov said sharply, "please. We are prepared to listen to your client's terms, Monsieur Léon."

Fredericks turned to Petkov.

"DIVADS," he said.

"What?"

"DIVADS," Fredericks repeated. "It's an acronym for Division Air Defense Gun System. It's a 'miss-distance' feedback fire control system for tactical antiaircraft use in the field. Within the next eight months NATO will make a choice between two systems currently being tested in the United States. One system, designed by Ford, uses twin forty-millimeter Bofors cannons. The other, designed by General Dynamics, uses twin thirty-five millimeter Oerlikons with proximity fuses. My client has written an article on the acceptance test criteria that will be used to determine the competition. Such an article, he feels, would be of particular interest, taking a hypothetical case, to planners trying to decide, say, what grade of plate to put on their tactical aircraft."

"And this...article...is also from the Lincoln Laboratory?" Petkov asked.

"Damned if I know how he does his research," Fredericks said cheerfully. "I can tell you the terms, though."

"Please."

"Ten thousand francs Swiss, the article. If you want this one, you're in for twenty."

Petkov did not hesitate, nor did he look at Yeremenko, which pleased Fredericks.

"I am sure, Monsieur Léon, that we would be able to place the article for such a price."

"You have a pen?" Fredericks asked.

"Yes." Petkov opened a small notebook.

"You have four days to deposit the twenty thousand francs," Fredericks said. "The bank is the Schweitzer Eigentums Bank. A.G., Paradplatz twelve, Zurich. The number of the account to which you will deposit the funds is 762 101 AE. You will ask for a Dr. Joseph Baer, to whom you must give my name before the deposit will be accepted. Is that clear?"

"Yes," Petkov said.

"Repeat it."

Petkov did so.

"Good," Fredericks said. "Within a week or ten days you will receive a call from me at your office. Be available there from nine to five. I will give you at that time an address, to which, within twenty minutes, you will bring *written* confirmation of the deposit. *Written,* is that clear? If everything else is satisfactory, you will then receive, or be directed to, the DIVADS article. Clear?"

"Yes." Petkov looked slightly uncomfortable. "I must tell you, Monsieur Léon, that my instructions are that all further contact with you will be made through Monsieur Yeremenko. It is for that purpose that he has been sent."

"Frankly, Gospodin Petkov," Fredericks said, "I don't give a damn whether it's you or someone else. All I'm concerned about is confirmation of the deposit."

An old woman carrying a wooden cigar box came scurrying up to them, demanding eighty centimes apiece for the use of the chairs. Petkov reached for his pocket, but Fredericks stopped him.

"My treat," he said, giving the woman a five-franc note as he rose. "I'll be looking behind me very carefully for the next few hours, Gospodin Petkov. If I make a tail, and I will if there is one, you'll never see me again. You understand?"

"I understand," Petkov said.

"I owe you," Yeremenko said, still sitting, his legs stretched before them, chewing at a nail as he looked up at Fredericks with his flat pig's eyes, "for the chair."

"Don't worry," Fredericks said. "You'll get a chance to pay."

Both men watched Fredericks impassively as he strolled unhurriedly into the shadows beneath the chestnut trees. He was a large man, his rolling gait distinctive, and the startling abruptness with which he was suddenly gone from view, Petkov decided, was simply a phenomenon of the light.

Fredericks recognized that it was not unnatural that he should wish to call Danielle, nor even that the longing should be so immoderate, intemperate.

He realized, of course, that he could not—*must* not—call, and thus, as solace, he allowed himself briefly to attempt to conjure her in familiar poses; bathing, brushing her hair, astride him in delight.

The only image that came, however, was of a door, wooden with a pebbled-glass partition, from behind which came soft and unbearably recognizable cries of anguish, and on which were stencilled the words:

M. BOURRELIER: INSPECTEUR PRINCIPAL

As the image flashed, Fredericks, walking in the rue Gay-Lussac, was suddenly bent double by an intense wave of pain. For a wild moment he feared himself shot, or ill, until the agony receded and he recognized the sensation, stirring after years of atrophy, for what it was: the gestation pains of Bourrelier's death, which he carried now in his guts, and which nothing could prevent him from bringing to term.

In the end, therefore, the call he made to Stuarti at the Taormina number that he had left was fortuitous.

Fredericks explained it to himself as normal tradecraft, "taking the temperature" in light of the surveillance to which Stuarti had recently been subject, since the alternative explanation—an unmastered desire, however unconscious, inchoate, to hear the sound of a familiar human voice—was unacceptable.

He placed the call from the cabin of a post office in the rue Claude-Bernard. The phone was answered on the third ring.

It was sloppily done; Fredericks guessed that the extension phone was in a separate room.

Asking for Mr. Stuarti, he was requested to hold. A full thirty seconds passed before another voice came on the line.

"Hello?" the voice said. The accent, though not Parisian, was clearly French.

"Edward?" said Fredericks.

"I'm sorry," the voice said, "Monsieur Stuarti

199

is unable to come to the phone at the moment. He asks that you leave a number at which he may call you back in ten minutes."

"Certainly," Fredericks said without hesitation. "In Paris, 202-51-00. Cabin number three."

"Thank you. He'll call you right back."

"Thank *you*." Fredericks hung up and left the post office.

He watched from a doorway next to a taxi stand two blocks distant. The speed was impressive. Within six minutes three unmarked cars, carrying four plainclothesmen each, had quietly pulled up in front of the post office. A Black Maria glided to a stop in a nearby side street and discharged a squad of uniformed policemen who immediately halted all pedestrian traffic on the street. As the plainclothesmen entered the post office, Fredericks entered the lead taxi in the rank, gave as a destination a street in the fifteenth arrondissement, and, as the cab turned into the rue Berthollet, was gone.

"Monsieur Cassin?" Fredericks said, calling that evening from the place Balard.

"Yes," Jean-Jacques Cassin said.

"It's your family friend," Fredericks said, "calling to make sure that your homework's all done."

"The loan has been arranged," Cassin said glumly. "The joint-tenancy papers are being drawn up and are to be ready Tuesday next."

"Tell me about the loan," Fredericks said.

"They would only go to straight cash value," Cassin said. "They assured me that that was the maximum possible."

"Well, you're probably lying," Fredericks said amiably, "but that doesn't much matter. We're still talking about some two hundred thousand dollars or so, yes?"

"Two hundred and eight thousand dollars," Cassin said, his voice strained.

"You O.K., Pumpkie?" Fredericks asked. "You sound a little nervous."

"A *little* nervous?" Cassin said. "I haven't slept for a week. I've had diarrhea every day since your visit."

"An irrelevant and distasteful detail, Pumpkie," Fredericks said. "Take some Lomotil and pull up your socks. Your little job's as easy as it could possibly be."

"Easy!" Cassin exclaimed.

"Sure. Let's go over your options, shall we? First, you could go take three weeks in the sun somewhere and pray like hell all this's just a bad dream, gonna be gone when you get back. That one won't work. I'll send the stuff to the papers, and when you get back you've gotta be a Fuller Brush man instead of a deputy. Unacceptable, agreed?"

"Yes," Cassin said.

"Second," Fredericks said, "you could go to the cops. Same problem there, plus it'd be very tough to find a charge on which to prosecute me. No good. Third, you could go to your brother. 'Some guy's blackmailing me to get to you. Help.' He'll make sure you haven't told anyone else, thank you for the warning, and three weeks later you'll bob up in the Seine somewhere around Issy-les-Moulineaux all blue and bloated with five slugs in your head, and I'll *still* send the stuff to the papers. So: me and him against you, you lose. You and him against me, well, better for him, but you still lose. But you and me against him, Pumpkie, and you walk away clean as a whistle. See how easy?"

"It's not easy at all," Cassin said crossly.

"A choice is always easy when it's the only one you've got. Do you have a pen?"

"Yes," Cassin said.

"I want you to arrange a meeting with your brother for next Friday, noon. Make it somewhere public...a bar, restaurant, whatever. Near the place Vendôme. I don't care what you have to tell him to get him to come, just do it."

"What if I can't?" Cassin whined.

"Then you start lugging a sample case full of toilet brushes and ringing doorbells," Fredericks said. "I'd try pretty hard, if I were you."

"That's Friday the third, at noon, place Vendôme area?" Cassin said.

"That's the spirit, Pumpkie. I'll be in touch."

No longer able to trust the Belgian identity papers that Stuarti had given him, Fredericks moved from the rue Pergolèse to a *hôtel de passe* near Gare du Nord, where twenty francs served as a welcomed substitute for an identity card.

He had five days to wait.

Although he was quite aware that within a week he would kill, and perhaps himself be killed, he felt neither apprehension nor anticipation, but rather an odd lassitude, an utter emptiness of affect.

On Saturday morning he shopped in a nearby market, buying a pound of sliced ham, a round loaf of dark country bread, and two bottles of Polish vodka.

He spent the weekend in his hotel room. Much of the time he simply sat in the room's single chair, weatherless, sipping from time to time from a glass of vodka. Occasionally, he would play a game of pitch-penny against the baseboard of the far wall. He was very good. Once he watched a portion of an automobile race on the room's antique television, another time a nature show called *"Monde des Animaux, Monde des Plantes."* Once he wondered whether Stuarti was still alive. He slept poorly, and guessed it was because he needed a woman.

In the dark, unbidden, the memories came.

Fredericks's *de facto* dismissal hearing—or rather, that brief portion of it for which Fredericks had remained—had taken place in a safe house in Saint-Ouen, a suburb to the south of Paris.

Two men had been there; Richardson, whose protegé Fredericks had been, and who Fredericks assumed had been flown to France in order to guarantee his return, and another man introduced to Fredericks as a Mr. Hazeltine.

"We shall assume you to be ill, Noah," Richardson had said. "There can be no other explanation...."

"Out of his fucking mind," Hazeltine had added.

"Tomorrow you and I return on a military flight from Roissy," Richardson continued, in a tone which suggested that they would share the same welcome, "but first there are some questions to which Mr. Hazeltine must have the answers."

"One question," Hazeltine said, "one answer. How did you know where to find Marićić? That's the question. The fat faggot who runs the safe house in Saint-Germain, that's the answer, only the Operations people want it to come from you."

It was a moment before Fredericks spoke; when he did, he offered not an answer, but a question of his own.

"What interest would Operations have in Maričić?" he asked.

"Four goddamned years of interest!" shouted Hazeltine, who was not deft, and had not done his homework for the meeting. "That's how long it took us to put him in place. And then you whack him out on your own initiative, like some huge Boy Scout gone nuts! Jesus Christ!..."

"Questions only, please," Richardson said, "we're in a hurry."

But it was too late.

"Four years?" Fredericks said, looking at his bandaged hand. He then looked up, held Richardson's eyes with his, and asked, "Four years?"

"One can't always choose one's sources," Richardson began, "nor judge their needs as they see them. You must under...."

Fredericks was already on his feet. "The expediency of temporary alliances? The sacrifice of the individual for the gain of the masses? Madison Avenue Leninism? From you?" His face was very white.

"Oh, for Christ's sake," Hazeltine said in disgust.

Fredericks put his uninjured hand on Hazeltine's shoulder and asked him to be quiet. Into that quiet he addressed his last words to Richardson.

"Shame on you, old man," Fredericks said.

He did not close the door behind him as he left.

On the Monday following his meeting with Richardson, Fredericks had submitted his resumé to a large executive recruitment firm in Puteaux. Specialists in system software were in high demand, and where a more exigent eye would have remarked a two-year hole in the resumé, indifferently papered over as post-graduate research, the eager recruiter to whom Fredericks spoke saw only "American" and "IBM"; both were enjoying momentary cachet in France. Fredericks was placed before the week was out, accepting the first offer made him.

That Saturday he met Danielle.

Fredericks's new employer, eager to please and more eager still to impress, had insisted that Fredericks accompany him to a French country weekend, hosted by the company's titled president at his private chateau in the Forest of Rambouillet. At dinner Danielle had sat to the host's left.

She was tall and blonde and utterly beautiful, violet-eyed and high cheek-boned, and was the only woman at the table of eight. She spoke only when directly addressed, and her indifference to the conversation was so transparent that their host once seemed on the point of irritation with her, until she drank from his glass, hers being empty, and in his pride he forgave her all.

Fredericks found her in the kitchen after dinner, nibbling choice leftovers from the plates and chatting comfortably with the cook.

"Did I understand you to say at dinner that you were a Thomist?" Fredericks asked.

"Tomiste," she said. "T.O.M. *Territoire d'Outre-Mer.* I was born in Guadeloupe."

"Ah," said Fredericks. "And your parents still live there?"

"My mother's dead," she said, inspecting the dessert plates.

"And your father?" Fredericks asked.

"Dead, too," she said. "Bite of *profiterolle?"* and

for the third time since they had been introduced their eyes met and held.

"No, thanks," Fredericks said.

"Where do you live?" she asked after a moment.

"In a hotel," Fredericks said.

"Where do you eat, then?" she asked, her tone that of one orphan discussing important logistics with another.

"In a restaurant in the rue du Dragon."

"I'd offer you some of this *paté de grives*," she said, when next she spoke, "but I think that the plate was Monsieur de Gramont's, and he has warts."

"Maybe next time, then."

"I always notice hands," she said.

"Important, an eye for detail," Fredericks said.

"Yours is all hurt," Danielle said.

Fredericks said nothing.

"Poor hand," she said, and then, ignoring the presence of the cook, she picked up his hand as though it were an injured bird and slipped it into her blouse, beneath her arm, for comfort and warmth.

Her armpit was shaven, smooth, and wet, and her breast against his palm was taut.

They slept together in what was clearly her room that night. The chateau was surrounded by woods, the silence profound, and she pressed her face into the pillow to muffle her love cries as she came, in deference to their host.

Fredericks had returned to Paris early the next morning, riding comfortably in frozen silence with his horrified employer.

That evening Danielle appeared at the restaurant in the rue du Dragon. She arrived as his coffee did, and Fredericks guessed that she had waited for him to finish his meal.

"Not only nature abhors a vacuum," she had said, sliding onto the banquette beside him. "Did you know that there are fourteen restaurants in the rue du Dragon?"

In the first months they made love whenever they were together, as though to preclude any possible confusion as to the nature of their relationship. Danielle spoke of Fredericks's penis as "he" and often addressed it directly, with a solicitousness more normally accorded adored pets or indulged children, explaining (in view of Fredericks's taciturnity) that it was nice to always have someone to talk to.

Later, Fredericks would read in the evenings after dinner—English language books which he ordered from Galignani—and Danielle would sew, an improbable skill taught her by the nuns as a substitute, she assumed, for faith.

Fredericks's books moved in first. When they filled three shelves. Fredericks, too, moved in.

Together they began to heal, which was enough, and they did not speak of love, ever.

In his room that night in the cheap hotel near the Gare du Nord. Fredericks saw Danielle standing before a cottage covered with primroses, an infant in pajamas on her shoulder sleeping with its face buried in her neck.

It was spring, the air liquor-rich with new fragrances, and Fredericks was saying goodby, he did not know why. When he held them in his arms the child smelled of milk and baby, Danielle of sweet sweat and sleep. Fredericks's feelings were of inexpressible tenderness, which made the child's voice, when it spoke, only the more horrific.

"You're ill, Noah," it said, and when Fredericks recoiled, in horror and protest, it turned its face to him, the features Laloux's even to the tiny glasses.

"Would you like to see the pictures?" it asked.

On Monday morning he shaved and dressed, and went shopping in the rue du Faubourg Saint-Martin. At a sporting goods store that specialized in mountaineering supplies he purchased eight feet of one-inch tubular nylon webbing, sixty feet of 9 mm. Perlon rope, a figure-eight descender, and a single oval carabiner clip with a spring-loaded gate. The sales clerk recommended a hotel in Chamonix, and gave Fredericks his business card to present for a discount.

Fredericks returned to the hotel in time for the afternoon television shows. The set in his room received only one channel. He watched *"Réponse à Tout," "Une Minute Pour Les Femmes," "Hebdo-Jeunes,"* and the sixteenth episode of a serial entitled *"Mon Oncle et Mon Curé."*

He woke in the night, weeping, but could not recall his dream. He bathed his face with cold water, slowly drank a glass of vodka, and when at dawn he lay down again he thought only of hiding places in the woods—behind dark trees, in shadowed declivities of shattered rock—and so relaxed, and slept.

On Tuesday he watched a quiz show called *"Des Chiffres et Des Lettres,"* which on that day featured the games *"Le mot le plus long"* and *"Le compte est bon."* The longest word attained was *"hypothécaire,"* meaning mortgaged. The correct sum was 137.

On Wednesday he placed a telephone call from a PTT in the boulevard Magenta to the Hotel zum Storchën in Zurich, making a reservation for the following night. The small hotel was a pleasant one, only steps from the Limat Quai, and Fredericks regretted briefly that the reservation was not for him.

And then it was Thursday.

Dirty Thursday.

EIGHTEEN

FREDERICKS AWOKE AT 4:30 A.M. It was still dark. He bathed and shaved in the room's small sink. He put on his shorts and an undershirt and removed the length of bright red tubular nylon webbing from its shopping bag. This he wrapped twice around his waist, securing it in front in a ring-bend knot and trimming the excess cleanly with a pocketknife. He made the bed neatly, and on it laid out the suit, shirt, socks, and tie that he would wear.

He also placed his briefcase, empty, on the bed. Into this he put the carefully coiled length of 9 mm. rope, the figure-eight descender, the oval carabiner clip, and a thin metal ruler calibrated in centimeters.

He removed the automatic pistol from the bottom of his suitcase and methodically inspected the firing and clip-feed mechanisms. When he was satisfied, he wrapped both in a shirt and placed the shirt in the briefcase.

At the sink he poured two ounces of vodka into a tumbler and filled it with tap water. The possibility of being shot made it unwise to eat, and he knew that the drink would palliate his hunger.

Sitting quietly in the room's single chair, the red nylon ribbon gay against his white undershirt, he looked for all the world like a Christmas gift waiting to be opened, as the dawn began to rise, fresh and rose, above the City of Light.

* * *

Winthrop Burnham woke feeling poorly. Although he had eaten a bouillabaisse heavy with garlic the evening prior, he realized that his troubled sleep and rumbling bowels were the product of nervousness, not mere indigestion.

Burnham detested the Thursday meetings with Cassin. Their regularity violated his concept of responsible tradecraft, and the illusion which he was obliged to foster—Cassin as master, Burnham as man—was a role he found deeply disagreeable. That Cassin did little to conceal the fact that he regarded Burnham more as a courier than as a case officer was an additional source of sharp and constant irritation.

There was also, he recognized, an element of fear; the knowledge that one day he might arrive at the rendezvous to find not Yves Cassin, but a group of cold-faced men from the DST—France's counterintelligence branch—with a short list of utterly unanswerable questions.

Simply formulating the thought was sufficient to send him immediately to the toilet.

For breakfast, Burnham had two cups of weak tea and a bowl of Total (regularly purchased at the embassy commissary), which eased his stomach somewhat. Putting on his suit jacket and picking up his briefcase, he glanced from the fourth floor windows into the street below. His two bodyguards—he had come to refer to them privately as Alphonse and Gaston—were at their now-customary posts, Alphonse reading a newspaper behind the wheel of the Simca, Gaston leaning against a fender at the other end of the block, doing something, it appeared, to his fingernails. They could not have been more obvious, thought Burnham, had they been naked. Leaving the apartment, Burnham checked the alarm system on the door and windows facing onto the balcony, carefully double-locked the Chubb cylinders of the front door behind him, and pressed the button to summon the elevator.

It was 9:10 A.M. when Winthrop Burnham emerged from his building. As he reached the sidewalk the parade quietly formed, Alphonse in front, Gaston behind, and together they strolled down the rue de l'Yvette toward the Métro Jasmin.

It was 9:14 when they reached the Métro. Alphonse entered first, then Burnham; finally, with a cursory look around, Gaston.

Watching from a small florist's shop on the opposite side of the avenue Mozart, Fredericks reflected, as the florist waxed eloquent on the virtues of the philodendron, that they could not have been more obvious had they been naked.

"You don't look well." Yves Cassin eased his car into the traffic in the rue du Ranelagh. "Are you ill?"

"I had a bouillabaisse last night at Prunier's," Burnham said. "Too much garlic, maybe. Maybe some bad fish, I don't know."

"Bad fish *chez* Prunier?" Cassin raised an eyebrow. "Never."

"Nice to know," Burnham said. "I feel better already."

"Frankly," Cassin said, "I can't imagine that they would abuse the garlic, either. With a larger menu, they would have two stars."

"Listen," Burnham said, "I take it all back about the bouillabaisse. This is clearly a latent response to something I ate in the States two years ago, all right?"

"There's a McDonald's on the Champs-Elysées now," Cassin said.

"Oh, Jesus," Burnham said.

"I hear that the milkshakes are quite good," Cassin said.

"You hear wrong," Burnham said. "What do you have for me?"

"Well," Cassin said slowly, "for one thing, we have our old *pédé* friend, Monsieur Stuarti, in protective custody in the boulevard Mortier."

Burnham's heart jumped. "Yes?"

"The car was found at Orly. A ticket agent recognized him from photographs."

"Probably not too tough," Burnham said. "He must weigh two-fifty, and he was probably wearing a goddamned dress. What'd he have to say?"

"He was in Sicily," Cassin said. "We had to bring him back in a private plane. He didn't want to come at all."

"Can't say as I blame him," Burnham said. "What'd he have to say?"

"So far, not too much. He admitted immediately that Fredericks had come to see him but said it was only to borrow money. We asked some more, and he added that they had talked a bit. He recalled your name and the name of a Colonel Laloux. He denies doing Fredericks any papers and says he has no idea where he is now. A polygraph confirmed that he is telling the truth about Fredericks's whereabouts but suggests that he is pulling my legs about the papers."

"Leg," Burnham said.

"Pardon?" Cassin said frostily.

"One leg," Burnham said. "Pulling someone's leg, not 'pulling someone's legs'."

"I've heard an Englishman say 'legs'," Cassin

said. "I imagine it's been altered in America, like 'lift' and 'elevator'."

"Fine," Burnham said, "have it your way. Is that all he had to say?"

"That's all he's had to say so *far*. But then, it's only been about seventy-two hours, and we've had him standing up for most of them. If he has anything else to say, he'll be saying it soon."

"I don't think I want to know about that part," Burnham said after a pause.

"As you like." Cassin looked briefly at Burnham with an expression of embarrassed surprise tinged with contempt, an expression with which a surgeon might regard a colleague who had just confessed an unmastered intolerance for the sight of blood. *"Entièrement comme vous voulez, mon brave,"* he said, patting Burnham's knee.

As Fredericks walked up the rue de l'Yvette toward Burnham's building he looked about him with distaste. There was nothing in this expensive *quartier* of the Paris that he loved, the Paris that lived, invisible, down alleyways, in courtyards, hidden behind peeling and leprous *portes-cochères, au fond de la cour, escalier D à gauche.* Even the great boulevards of the Second Empire and the straight and confident streets of the Third Republic alarmed him with the discontinuity of their history. This portion of the sixteenth arrondissement could, as easily, have been Riverdale.

Everything about him he saw as through a pane of clear glass. The street noises seemed muffled to a point where Fredericks felt slightly deaf.

He wondered how far the interrogators had gotten with Stuarti. Stuarti was a professional and artful dissembler, and if the interrogators were proceeding at a leisurely pace he could put them through a series of hoops that could take days. Were they proceeding less leisurely, the lobby of Burnham's building could even now contain an additional brace of SDECE agents with instructions to shoot him dead on sight.

With an insouciant step and a jaunty *bonjour* for the gardener, Fredericks turned from the sidewalk and approached the front door of Burnham's building.

A low interior wall planted with greenery separated the entranceway from the lobby of Burnham's building. Beyond the wall there was the elevator, a single low couch of chrome and imitation leather, and the bank of mailboxes—eight in all—that testified to the absence of a resident concierge. Burnham's apartment, as Stuarti had reported, was No. 4-B.

The lobby was empty.

Fredericks pressed the elevator button. There was a soft thud and then the whirring hum of machinery as it descended.

The elevator, too, was empty.

There was no answer to his ring at the door of 5-B. The shuffle of footsteps and a woman's *"Qui est là?"*; however, followed his ring at the door of 6-B.

"Building insurance, Madame," Fredericks replied, occupation being far more reassuringly impersonal than a name.

The door was opened by a very black maid dressed in a white uniform. Fredericks guessed her to be Senegalese.

"Bonjour, Madame," Fredericks said.

"Bonjou'," the maid said.

Briskly, Fredericks explained that recently promulgated municipal regulations required the installation of a fire escape on the rear of the building, and that, as the representative of the building's insurance company, it was his responsibility to determine the feasibility of such an installation. Specifically, he explained, he was to evaluate the possible means of egress to the building's rear. He spoke very quickly, in the distinctive sing-song of the French functionary.

"*Il n'y a qu'un petit fenet' dans la cuisine,*" said the maid, her features clearly troubled by the heretofore unconsidered logistical problems involved in maneuvering her substantial haunches through a small window in the kitchen in order to escape an unspeakable death by fire.

Exactly, Fredericks agreed grimly, and if he might just measure?

The maid, understandably, did not ask for identification; Fredericks's suit, tie, briefcase, and bearing were far more legitimizing than any business card could ever have been.

Fredericks's inspection of the kitchen window was professionally brief; it opened inward, was sufficiently large to permit the passage of a man's body, and was secured only by a simple handle. Opening it and peering outward, Fredericks noted with satisfaction that there was such a window on each of the floors beneath.

Opposite, the partially completed apartment building of which Stuarti had spoken dominated a lot littered with construction debris. Whether because of the inevitable labor difficulties, or the absence of completion financing, construction on the building had been halted. The reinforcing steel rods protruding from the foundation concrete were rusted; the rainwater that had pooled in an abandoned wheelbarrow was scummed with algae. As he looked very carefully, the only movement that Fredericks noticed was that of a nondescript black dog which, in the absence of contravening authority, had opportunistically converted a large pile of construction sand into an admirably commodious *pissoir*.

Thanking the maid for her assistance, Fredericks allowed himself to be shown to the door. Regaining the hall, Fredericks bowed gravely, bid the woman good day, and then, as an afterthought, said, "Oh, yes, we'll be measuring on the roof and on the wall facing. We hope the noise, if any, won't disturb you unduly."

The absence of a visible colleague in no way vitiated Fredericks's "we," for in France the voice of authority speaks with the plural pronoun.

In a tone that suggested that, if Fredericks's efforts could possibly reconvert the deathtrap in which she now worked into the luxury apartment it had been prior to his visit, no inconvenience would be too heavy to bear, the maid assured Fredericks that she would not be troubled by whatever noise such work entailed.

Fredericks now moved quickly. He closed the fire door to the roof quietly behind him and crossed the gravel to a heavy iron exhaust pipe that protruded five feet from the surface of the roof. There he knelt and opened his briefcase. From it he withdrew the sixty feet of Perlon rope, the figure-eight descender, and the oval carabiner.

Where he had marked the center of the rope with a piece of tape he formed a bight which he fed first into the top circle of the metal descender, then passed around the shank separating the two circles, repassed it again through the top of the descender, and secured it over the exhaust pipe. Crossing to the edge of the roof, he threw the two loose ends over. They snaked down the side of the building, dangling twelve feet or so past Burnham's kitchen window.

Fredericks undid two buttons on the front of his shirt and clipped the red nylon webbing around his waist into the carabiner. He then clipped the handle of his briefcase into the carabiner, and, finally, the bottom circle of the figure-eight descender.

He leaned against the rope to test the system, then, without hesitation, stepped up onto the low retaining parapet and then, backward, into space.

Wearing a neatly pressed suit, his briefcase dangling at his side, he rappelled rapidly down the vertical wall. Had people seen him, they would simply have failed to credit their eyes, or—the *quartier* being a financially sophisticated one—assumed him, perhaps, to be an IOS salesman making a particularly difficult close.

The thin metal ruler easily opened the window to the kitchen. It was 9:38 A.M. as Fredericks stepped into Burnham's sink.

"Commercial ciphers!" Yves Cassin exclaimed with disgusted incredulity as they drove down the Quai de Grenelle. "That's all you've got for me, *commercial ciphers?*"

"Plus the modalities governing their use within the jurisdictional area of Paris station. Listen, if you really want high-level classified Agency material, why don't you take out a subscription to *Covert Action,* or whatever the hell it's called. I'm supposed to be a turned case officer. I can only

give you what a case officer would have access to. This week's flavor is commercial ciphers and modalities. That's it."

"May I remind you, Mr. Burnham," Cassin said with infuriating hauteur, "that I am the one at risk here, not you."

"As often as you like," Burnham said. "And you don't even *need* to remind me that you're the one getting paid, not me. What've you got for us?"

After a moment's clenched silence, Cassin produced the usual small film cassettes from his suit coat pocket. "Strategic Material Reserve Estimates," he said, "revised to current as of 31 March. They cover cobalt, titanium, chromium, manganese, copper, and molybdenum. The numbers refer to metric tons; the first number is 'on-hand' estimates; the second, committed deliverables."

"Provenance indicated for the deliverables?" Burnham asked, as he put the cassettes into his briefcase.

"Mr. *Burnham!*" Cassin said, sarcastically guying injured feelings as they turned onto the Pont du Garigliano. "Do we seem the sort of people who would do business with South Africa?"

As Fredericks did not know how much time he had before Burnham's return, his initial inspection of the apartment was cursory.

It was the windowless master bathroom that pleased him most, for while the shaving kit on the sink and the socks soaking in the bidet were normal enough, the developing tank with a large red, safety light, brown bottles of developer, fixer, and hypo fluid, an editor with an illumination screen for reading negatives, and a shiny new electric timer on the enamel table next to the tub were reassuringly less usual appointments.

The bathroom opened from the single hallway that led to the bedroom, the kitchen, and Burnham's study. Fredericks opened his briefcase. Into it he placed the neatly recoiled rope, and from it he withdrew the automatic pistol and its clip.

He slid the clip into place with a soft click, he closed the bathroom door until it was barely ajar, as he had found it, and in the darkness, breathing with a soft and utterly inappropriate calmness, he waited.

Yves Cassin dropped Burnham at the corner of the rue de l'Yvette and the rue du Docteur-Blanche. Walking down the street toward his building, Burnham was conscious of a new heaviness to the sun's heat, an augury of the sullen summer dog days to come.

As he passed the car in which Gaston impassively sat, he noticed that the man was probing vigorously in his ear with his forefinger. As Burnham watched, he withdrew the finger, examined with intent scrutiny the product obtained beneath the nail, and then, satisfied with his examination, sucked the nail clean. Burnham's biliousness, which the interview with Cassin had done little to palliate, rose and redoubled.

The morning's post had brought only bills and advertisements. There was, however, a two-day-old *Wall Street Journal,* and as Burnham entered the elevator it was his highest ambition to regain the cool privacy of his apartment, there to relieve his troubled bowels and peruse in peace the financial quotations reporting Monday's close.

Burnham carefully double-locked the door behind him, cursorily checked the alarm system monitoring the balcony doors and windows, and gratefully removed his suit coat, tossing it onto the couch. Loosening his trousers and glancing at the front page of the *Journal*, he passed to the bathroom.

What happened next happened, it seemed to Burnham, with a speed that had no place in time.

As he reached absently for the light switch, he was suddenly aware of a faint smell of sweat not his own. As suddenly, an iron hand closed on his throat, lifting him effortlessly from the floor and slamming him like a rag doll against the wall.

Burnham, understandably, was ill-prepared for the presence of something large and violent in his bathroom.

Adrenaline struck his system like a heart attack.

The Wall Street Journal fluttered to the bathroom floor from his splayed and rigid fingers.

A thin stream of excrement slid down his leg.

Even had the hand on his throat permitted, he could not have made a sound.

Fredericks's face was utterly expressionless as he slowly raised the pistol and gently pressed the muzzle of the gun between Burnham's bulging eyes.

"I have some questions, Mr. Burnham," he said.

When Fredericks's hand left his throat, the blood roared into Burnham's ears like a black tide and amoebas of light flashed and receded in an otherwise utter darkness before his open eyes. He was conscious of a sense of falling, then of floating, and finally of a small and very distant pain as his bony spine struck an unyielding surface.

Slowly the roar in his ears gave over to a rasping sound, which he identified as breathing before he realized it to be his own, and then, quite suddenly and with startling clarity, he found himself sitting on the toilet in his semi-darkened bathroom, Fredericks's hand on his shoulder holding him hard against the porcelain tank. Placing the muzzle of the pistol beneath Burnham's chin, Fredericks raised Burnham's eyes to meet his own. Even in the half-light, Burnham was appalled by what he saw.

"First question," Fredericks said, very quietly. "Is there a recording system in the apartment, and if so, is it on?"

"No," Burnham whispered.

"No which, you son of a bitch?" Fredericks breathed.

"There isn't any."

"Good," Fredericks said. "Second question. Are you supposed to wave at your sitters or anything, let 'em know there wasn't anything nasty in the bathroom when you got home?"

"No."

"You're quite sure about that? Keeping in mind that if anybody comes through that door, he gets shot *second.*"

"I'm sure." Burnham was still whispering as though to avoid calling undue attention to himself.

"Good. What time are you expected at the Embassy signal room?"

"What?"

The barely perceptible noise of the pistol's safety being eased off obliterated all other sounds, leaving them together in a vast silence.

"In Belgrade, in the spring," Fredericks said,

"the cottonwood trees give off their spores, and for a week or two the air of the city is filled with tiny, white, weightless puffs, floating everywhere. Even indoors, you find them in your soup, in your wine.

"Four years ago this month I picked up a suit from a cleaner's in Washington and discovered the things still in the pockets, still clinging to the linings of the sleeves. I found it...objectionable... that these ephemeral seeds should have outlived men and women whose only—and fatal—error was to believe that a loyalty declared was a loyalty given."

Fredericks here began to tremble slightly as he spoke, which frightened Winthrop Burnham very, very much.

"You see, Mr. Burnham, loyalty matters. Particularly to the dead, Mr. Burnham, who can look only to the living for justice. And that there are wrongs which are *blood* wrongs is a wisdom ancient, not antique. To allow..."

Suddenly Fredericks was no longer trembling, but shaking, hard. He breathed deeply, desperately, his breath whistling in his bared teeth.

Even in fear of death, Burnham was appalled by the iron effort of black will with which Fredericks brought himself again to control.

"To allow betrayal to become acceptable, Mr. Burnham," continued Fredericks with the tight inexorability of a man determined to finish his sentence and then be done with words, "is to damage the social organism far more seriously than it would be were it to be diminished by one aging, incompetent, incontinent cell. On which grounds, my friend, I'll blow your fucking face right off the front of your head the next time you even *think* about hedging an answer. *What time are you expected at the Embassy signal room?"*

"Before two o'clock if there's a hard product for the bag. Before three if I want same day encoding and transmission," Burnham said quickly, praying for another question more urgently than he had ever prayed for anything in his life.

His prayer was answered, brutally.

"How do you pay Yves Cassin?"

Burnham slumped as though he had been struck. Whatever exiguous will to resist there had been was broken, utterly.

"Cash transfers to a Zurich bank," he said, addressing the floor.

"Names and numbers, please." Fredericks removed a small notebook from his jacket pocket.

Dully, Burnham told him everything.

"I also need to know everything he's given you," Fredericks said, still writing. "Topics, general level of detail, document classification and provenance, file numbers and cross-references...*you* know, Mr. Burnham."

Without pausing, Burnham slowly listed for Fredericks the products that Cassin had provided. Given the circumstances, his retention of detail was impressive.

"Last question," Fredericks asked. "Where's today's product?"

"In my briefcase. The combination is six-two-two. Three film cassettes. Don't kill me." His bowels rumbled again as he began to weep.

"Christ," Fredericks said in disgust, "a man had the Kaopectate concession in this business he could get rich quick. Here's what you do, Mr. Burnham. You wash, get dressed, and pack an overnight bag. Then you call the Embassy, tell 'em no product today, you won't be in. Then you call your office, tell 'em you're taking a long weekend, see 'em Monday. You do all those things just right, you just might live to shit on somebody else besides yourself again. Where do you keep the vodka?"

"In the living room, on the sideboard," Burnham whimpered.

"Make it quick," Fredericks said.

When Burnham emerged from the bedroom still very pale but somewhat more composed, Fredericks was sitting in an armchair next to the extension phone. A bottle of Stolichnaya, which Burnham had just purchased the day before, stood on the wing table next to him.

"Nice suit," Fredericks said.

"Thank you," Burnham said.

"Sit down."

Burnham sat down.

"Now pay attention, all right? There's a happy ending here, or an unhappy ending, and the choice's up to you. You have a reservation for this evening at the Hotel zum Storchën in Zurich. Know it?"

"Yes," Burnham said.

"Good. You go there this afternoon. Drive, fly, whatever suits you. You have a few glasses of Fendant, a nice dinner, a good night's sleep. Tomorrow around noon, you'll get a call at the hotel from Yves Cassin. With the information he'll give you, you pick up some money—cash—from two banks, and you deposit it in a third. That's it. Cassin's going to lose a little money, you'll probably lose him as an agent, but that's all. That's the happy ending.

"Or," Fredericks continued, "you don't do it.

228

Instead of going to Zurich, you run straight to Cassin, or Blaine, or whoever. In which case Cassin goes to jail, the newspapers have a field day, agents you've never even heard of start jumping ship, and you spend the rest of your life wearing Pampers and looking over your shoulder for me. And one fine day, Mr. Burnham, just like today, I'll be there. That's the unhappy ending. Got a preference?"

Burnham cleared his throat. "The happy one. I prefer the happy one."

"Sound thinking, Mr. Burnham. Most impressive demonstration I've seen from you so far. Almost enough to restore one's confidence in the acuity of the legal mind. Where do you keep your car?"

"It's in the garage, downstairs."

"Your sitters know it?"

"Yes," Burnham said.

"Got a large screwdriver?"

"Yes," Burnham said, "it's in the kitchen closet."

"Get it," Fredericks said. "Then leave some lights on and bring your little bag."

Together they descended in the elevator to the garage beneath Burnham's building.

Fredericks chose a metallic-blue, four-year-old Renault 16 TS.

Slipped down along the window, the thin metal ruler opened the door within ten seconds.

Fredericks lodged the heavy screwdriver in the ignition and struck it once, hard, with the heel of his hand. The ignition cylinder popped out the back of the dashboard and hung above the brake, dangling from its wires. Fredericks jerked the wires loose from the cylinder, examined them briefly, then touched two together. The car started immediately.

Alphonse and Gaston gave the car no more than a cursory glance as they reached the street and turned away toward the avenue Mozart.

Ten minutes later they abandoned the car in a parking garage at the Porte Maillot.

"There's a Hertz office in the place Saint-Ferdinand," Fredericks said, "about a three-minute walk from here. Think you can find it without getting lost?"

"Yes," Burnham said.

"Good boy. Have a nice trip, and mind how you go. Can't be too careful."

It was Burnham who started walking first.

Slowly, initially, then with more speed.

When at last he dared a glance behind him, Fredericks was gone.

NINETEEN

FREDERICKS CALLED FROM a café in the place du Pérou, a five-minute walk from the apartment in the rue Murillo that he had rented in Yves Cassin's name.

Jean-Jacques Cassin's number in the rue Théodule Ribot was at first busy.

While he waited, Fredericks watched an elderly man in blue work clothes with a paste bucket and leveling board plastering pharmaceutical advertisements on the wall opposite the cafe.

Monsieur! read the first strip. *C'est VOUS le coupable si Madame est frigide!*

The old man leaned backward, regarded the grim assertion glumly, and began plastering the back of the second strip.

Fredericks dialed the number again. The phone rang half-a-dozen times without response.

Prenez, donc, du tonique FORTIFEX! read the second strip.

Jean-Jacques answered on the tenth ring.

"Allô, oui?" he said cautiously.

"Christ, Pumpkie," Fredericks said, "I was beginning to think that maybe you'd reconsidered and chosen three weeks in the sun."

"I was in the bathroom," Cassin said coldly.

"Stop!" Fredericks said sternly. "I don't want to hear about it. Is the appointment with your brother set?"

"Noon tomorrow. We're to meet in the garden bar of the Hotel Continental."

"What'd you tell him?"

"I told him that I was being blackmailed by a family friend."

"Well," Fredericks said. "That should've gotten his attention."

"I'd like to ask a favor, if I might." Cassin cleared his throat.

"Certainly."

"I would appreciate it," Cassin said, "if you would *not* call me 'Pumpkie' tomorrow."

"Mais ne vous inquiétez pas, mon cher Monsieur le Député," said Fredericks, "certain occasions, like blackmailing one's brother, impose their own dignity. *A demain.*"

He rang off.

Vyacheslav Petkov answered his telephone much more quickly than Cassin.

"This is Monsieur Léon," Fredericks said without preamble. "Do you have written confirmation of the deposit?"

"Yes," Petkov said. "We were beginning to worry that we weren't going to hear from you."

"Yeremenko have his track shoes on?" Fredericks asked.

"Monsieur Yeremenko is here, yes," Petkov said.

"There's a café in the place du Pérou, in the eighth," Fredericks said. "It's on the western side of the *place,* called *Au Bon Accueil.* There's a public telephone downstairs, next to the toilets. Twenty minutes from now it's going to ring. Yeremenko's to answer, identifying himself by name. He'll get further instructions then. He's to come alone and unwired. He'll be watched from the minute he leaves the bank. If there's a tail, it'll be made. Understood?"

"Monsieur Léon," Petkov began, "could you repeat...."

"No," Fredericks said. "Play it back if you need to. He's got twenty minutes."

As Fredericks left the café, the old man was putting up the first strip of another advertisement on a newly scraped portion of wall adjacent to the *Fortifex* poster.

Madame! it read. *Avez-vous les maux de têtes?*

Fredericks walked north, his briefcase in his hand.

As is always the case with such artificially furnished rooms, the air of specious luxury attempted in the apartment in the rue Murillo failed to cloak an essential, soulless anonymity. No appointment had been chosen with a loving eye, and a pervasive floral odor of commercial disinfectant substituted for, rather than masked, those smells of tobacco, food, night sweat, and love acid, which in a home reassuringly suggest the human.

Fredericks allowed twenty-five minutes to pass before he dialed the number of the public telephone in the café.

"Arvid Yeremenko," said the voice that Fredericks clearly recalled, in a slow, bored bully's drawl.

"Leave the café without making any further calls," Fredericks said, speaking slowly. "Turn left out the front door of the café and walk north on the rue Rembrandt for two blocks, to the rue Murillo. Walk quickly and don't look back. When you reach the rue Murillo, turn right to Number Twelve. Ring the buzzer for apartment Seven-C. If we like what we see, you'll be buzzed in. If not, don't bother to wait. Is that clear?"

"Yes," Yeremenko said. "Stupid, of course, unnecessary, but clear."

Fredericks hung up.

Fredericks closed all the doors leading to the sitting room. He checked the locks on the double-glazed windows, then drew the heavy drapes. He put his briefcase on a low coffee table in front of the couch that faced the door.

He opened the briefcase, its top toward the door. He arranged the pistol neatly on the coil of rope which he had used that morning at Burnham's apartment. He glanced at a print on the wall, a bright scene of mountains and skaters, of *sport d'hiver,* and thought to himself—though it was but April—winter soon. Then he said it out loud.

"Winter soon," he said.

The buzzer sounded.

Glancing at his watch, Fredericks noticed with regret that he had already missed that day's emission of *"Monde des Animaux, Monde des Plantes."*

When the knock came, Fredericks was sitting on the couch, one foot up on the low coffee table, facing the door.

"It's open," he shouted, quite loudly.

There was no response, which pleased him.

There was another knock, and then the handle of the door turned, slowly. When it had opened six inches, Fredericks spoke again. "Come in."

The door opened, and Yeremenko's squat bulk was silhouetted against the light-blue, flocked wallpaper of the hall, his hands empty.

"You are alone, Monsier Léon?" he said.

"Yes," Fredericks said. "Close it, and lock it."

Yeremenko did so. When he turned to face Fredericks, his expression was mocking.

"Cowboys et Peaux-Rouges, you call this, yes?" he said contemptuously. "Next time, we do this another way."

"Do you have the deposit slip?" Fredericks asked.

Yeremenko withdrew an envelope from his jacket pocket and waggled it in his thick fingers.

"Put it on the sideboard, over there," Fredericks said.

Yeremenko strolled to the far corner of the room and tossed the envelope onto the sideboard. When he turned again to speak. Fredericks was holding the pistol in his right hand, bracing it lightly with his left. It was pointed directly between Yeremenko's eyes.

"On your stomach," Fredericks said, "hands straight out."

Yeremenko's lips curled. "You want also my taxi money, Monsier Léon?"

"No," Fredericks said, "I'm going to tie you hand and foot, fill your pockets with embarrassing things, and leave you here for collection. Move."

"I bring you money, you point a gun at me," Yeremenko said woefully, putting his hands on his hips and shaking his head, a man of good will saddened, rather than angered, by the boundless perfidy of the West.

Beneath the skirt of his jacket, six inches from his hand, the butt of a pistol showed, quite clearly.

Yeremenko's thick legs tensed.

Fredericks fired.

The bullet struck Yeremenko squarely in the brow, just beneath the hairline, and tore off the top of his head.

Shards of brain tissue spattered the wall behind him. A single, large piece of skull detached itself as if in slow motion, struck the wall in a lazy arc, and came to rest on the carpet, rocking slightly.

With short, colorless hair on the outside, and an inside of gleaming, white, bloodless bone, it looked very much like a piece of freshly broken coconut.

Before the first, flat echo of the shot had slapped back to him, Fredericks was crouching behind the low coffee table, the pistol trained on the door, his arm rigid. A full thirty seconds passed before he moved.

He rose slowly, removed the clip from the butt of the gun, and replaced both in the briefcase. Using a handkerchief, he removed from the briefcase those film cassettes that he had taken from Burnham and an envelope containing a neatly typed list of Yves Cassin's products.

Fredericks crossed to the body that had been Yeremenko. Where before there had been a man in a suit, now there was merely a huddled pile of meat and laundry.

"It's just a mistake to think that history's only on your side," Fredericks said, looking down. "My father, for instance, couldn't even hit a ball with a bat."

The sound of his speech startled Fredericks. Neither the voice nor the words seemed to be his own.

He knelt and placed the film cassettes in Yeremenko's outside jacket pocket. After pressing the envelope several times against Yeremenko's fingertips and thumb, he placed it in the right-inside jacket pocket.

He closed the briefcase and stood, still looking down. When he spoke again, it was simply out of duty to an utterly unattainable clarity. "I mean, when he tried to bat right-handed, he'd always put his left hand on *top....*"

As he left the room, he became aware of a softer smell beneath the acridity of cordite, a rich smell of blood warmth, new skin, and a sly, corrupt hint of fecal sweetness.

It was not until he emerged into the empty hallway, carefully locking the door behind him, that he recognized it as the smell of the nursery, the odor of child.

In the night Fredericks walked, his legs leading him.

Once, somewhere in the thirteenth, there was the shop window of a *coutellerie,* knife blades gleaming in the weak light of a street lamp and on the door a *pancarte* reading *"Fermé pour cause de décés."*

Once, perhaps before, perhaps after, for sequence was elusive in the solitary dark in which he walked, in the sad and dying *quartier de Gergovie* beneath the looming mass of Maine-Montparnasse, a beggar to whom he gave a coin whispered horrifyingly, *"Moi aussi, je faisais mon service militaire á l'étranger."*

And once, somewhere north of the sad desert that had been the Halles, a silent woman in a doorway stared at him with eyes that had no color. The sign beside her read, *"Madame Irma. Passé. Présent. Avenir. Tarifs Humanitaire."*

Finally, in the alleys and *ruelles* of the *quartier de la Goutte d'Or* beneath the Butte-Montmartre, a quarter that had been a daily and nightly killing-ground during the Algerian war, Fredericks stopped in a small and nameless Algerian café.

There he sat, drinking slowly and waiting, as the night turned slowly colorless and became dawn.

When at last he stepped into the street that gave the quarter its name, a sick red sun was rising, painting the hideous basilica of Sacre-Coeur above him in *lie de vin*, the color of dried blood.

TWENTY

FREDERICKS MADE HIS remaining calls from a public telephone outside the Métro Palais Royale.

The conversation with Vyacheslav Petkov was brief.

"Dead?" Petkov asked.

"Yes."

"And is it your intention to keep the money?" Petkov's tone was conversational.

"Yes."

"You've made a very bad mistake, Monsier Léon. My firm will be angry."

As he hung up, Fredericks reflected that indeed they would be.

Fredericks's other calls—to the DST, the Gendarmerie Nationale, the newspaper *Le Canard Enchainé,* and *Agence France-Presse*—were only slightly longer, as Fredericks carefully explained to each respondent where Yeremenko's body might be located, the nature of the documents to be found on the body, and the disturbing implications of such documents for French security.

As he replaced the phone and turned away, Fredericks calculated that while it might take some time to establish the lessee of the apartment in which Yeremenko lay, to determine the holder of the Swiss account indicated by the deposit slip, and, most importantly, to develop the film, a comparison of the product list in Yeremenko's pocket with the access records of the relevant files should be completed within the hour.

Across the rue de Rivoli, the gleaming facade of the Hôtel Intercontinental shone brightly in the midday sun.

Yves Cassin ordered a Campari and soda. Jean-Jacques Cassin ordered a Scotch and milk. When the waiter left them, Yves regarded his younger brother proprietarily for a long moment, then said, "You look terrible."

"I *feel* terrible," Jean-Jacques said. "You think I order a whisky and milk for the taste?"

"What's wrong?"

"The doctor says I've developed a spastic colon," said Jean-Jacques. "Not that the goddamned thing was a monument to coordination before."

"It's nerves," Yves said. "Nerves do that."

"Is that right?" Jean-Jacques lit a cigarette with shaky hands. "You would've made a hell of a diagnostician. I suppose we can console ourselves that medicine's loss was the nation's gain."

"Calm down," Yves said. "You said on the telephone that you had a little problem?"

"Did I say 'little'?" Jean-Jacques asked. "I couldn't have said 'little.' Nothing little about it."

"A woman? Somebody threatening to call Marie-Claire and tell all?"

"A woman, *merde!*" Jean-Jacques said. "What am I going to do with a woman? Do you have any *idea* what a spastic colon can do to your sex life?"

"I can guess, thank you," Yves said with distaste. "What is it, then?"

"Since you're the master-guesser, why don't *you* give it a try?"

"You're in trouble with the land syndication in Saint-Lô," Yves said. "That it?"

"Congratulations, Monsieur Cassin," Jean-Jacques snarled. "You win the canned ham."

"I told you that you were going to get in trouble with that."

"I don't remember that. I remember that you said you didn't want any, but I don't remember you saying anything about trouble."

"I did."

"Maybe you did," Jean-Jacques said. "I don't remember it. I'm pretty sure, though, that you forgot to tell me that you were the one who was gonna *get* me in trouble with it. That part I would've remembered, had you said it."

Yves Cassin leaned forward. "What are you talking about?"

"Let's not sit too close, all right?" Jean-Jacques moved his chair and glanced nervously about.

"Explain yourself," Yves Cassin said sharply.

"Now wait a *minute*. I'm the one who's supposed to say that."

"Now," Yves said.

Jean-Jacques drew himself up in his chair. "I have reason to believe," he said, in a sonorous attempt at dignity undermined by an inadequately suppressed belch, "that you have betrayed me to foreign powers."

"And what reason would that be, pray?" Yves asked icily.

"That one," Jean-Jacques said glumly, pointing over his brother's shoulder.

When Yves Cassin turned his head, his eyes were level with Fredericks's belt buckle, perhaps two inches away.

"Bonjour, Colonel Laloux," Fredericks said.

*   *   *

Yves Cassin's head jerked up. Fear brought him halfway to his feet.

Fredericks's thick hand on his neck reseated him.

"Move again and I'll break your neck," Fredericks said, smiling amiably, a playful friend among friends.

"I have two men outside." Cassin's face was suddenly leached of color. "You...."

"Orthopedic specialists, are they?" Fredericks said.

"You are in very grave trouble," Cassin attempted, sweat beginning to bead on his lip.

"It's your brother *I'm* worried about." Fredericks seated himself and draped a comradely arm over Cassin's shoulders. "He's looking poorly, surely you agree?"

Yves Cassin said nothing. Jean-Jacques studiously removed an ice cube from his milk, an operation requiring his full attention.

"Depressed, is my guess," Fredericks continued. "I don't think I've seen him smile since I've known him. Exogenous depression, that's the one where there's a good reason, right?"

"I wouldn't know," Cassin said.

"Well, he's certainly got a reason, hasn't he? I mean the poor guy puts together this wonderful deal, pulls it off neat as you please, and then, out of the clear blue sky, *I* come along, thanks to you, and take away his two hundred grand. And since he's already *spent* it, in order to serve his country more fully, that leaves him in the hole to Crédit Lyonnais for the whole two hundred. No money, and God knows what kind of problems with the

Fisc, the way you've been talking. Wouldn't *you* be depressed?"

"What do you want?" Cassin blotted his lips and swallowed.

"We've got to cheer him up," Fredericks said, "and I think I've got just the ticket. First, let's convert the title to the Saint-Lô property to joint tenancy. Your official position should obviate any excessive zeal on the part of the Fisc at tax time, so that's *one* less worry. Second, you give him two hundred grand so that he can pay back Crédit Lyonnais. He'd probably feel most secure if you were a cosignatory to the loan. That way he can be sure he'll be able to find you when he needs you. What do you think? It's only fair, after all. If it hadn't been for you he never would have met me and had all these nasty things happen to him."

"You want me to give him two hundred thousand dollars?" Cassin smiled lightly.

"Well," Fredericks said, "it's actually *me* you're giving it to, but that's the general idea. I believe that you have the necessary papers, *Monsieur le Député?*"

Jean-Jacques lifted his briefcase from beneath his chair and began to withdraw the documents.

"You knew?" Yves asked his brother.

"One must protect oneself," Jean-Jacques responded archly. "You sign next to the blue x's."

"Petit salaud!"

"Vieux con!"

"Now, boys," Fredericks said, "each unhappy family is unhappy in its own way, and I'm afraid that, as partners, you're going to have to live with each other for a while. Let's just get the papers signed, *d'accord?*"

When the formalities were completed, Jean-Jacques stood.

"You want cash, Monsieur Cassin," Fredericks said. "One-hundred- and five-hundred-franc notes. Hurry back. We'll be right here."

Alone at the table they sat in silence, Fredericks's pale eyes holding Cassin in a gaze devoid of expression. When at last Fredericks spoke his eyes did not waver from Cassin's.

"Is Stuarti still alive?" he asked.

Although Fredericks's tone was as expressionless as his face, there was in the question both an assumption and a promise, and Cassin became aware of an actual physical chill as he realized that he was very close, indeed, to death.

"Yes," he said carefully.

Fredericks called the waiter and requested that a telephone be brought to the table. He did not speak again until it arrived.

"Call," Fredericks said, holding Cassin's eyes as he tapped the telephone. "Have him brought here. Now. If he's not here in thirty minutes, I'll assume you to be lying."

Without a word of protest Cassin made the call. He was emphatic in stressing to his respondent the necessity for haste, ordering that an ambulance be used.

When he hung up, Fredericks spoke again.

"Mr. Burnham is in Zurich," he said, "and expecting a call from you. You will instruct him to withdraw funds from two banks and transfer them to a third. The first account will be your own. He's to withdraw those funds you've received from him. Explain to him the necessary withdrawal modalities." Here Fredericks removed a piece of paper from his suit jacket. "The second," he continued, passing Cassin the paper, "is the top account written here. He is to identify himself to a Dr. Joseph Baer as acting as agent for a Monsieur Léon. The Handelsbank account is the one to which he is to deposit the funds from the other two. Is that clear?"

"The third account..." Cassin said, "...that would be yours?"

"Does it matter?"

There was an edge to Fredericks's voice that seemed, chillingly, to invite protest or refusal.

Cassin carefully offered neither.

The first time he dialed the number of the Hotel zum Storchën the lines were busy.

The second time they were clear.

"Darf ich bitte mit Herr Winthrop Burnham *sprechen?"* Cassin asked.

Cassin's conversation with Winthrop Burnham was brief; its content limited to banking detail, its tenor uncordial. At its close, perhaps in response to a remark that sounded to Fredericks, listening on the *écouteur,* very much like "I told you so," Cassin allowed himself a brief moment of frank acrimony, snarling "Ass's hole!" and hanging up before Burnham could correct his idiom.

"That's 'asshole'," Fredericks said. "We translate *'trou de cul'* as 'asshole'."

Thus when Jean-Jacques returned, he found Fredericks and his brother much as he had left them; Fredericks sipping a whisky, humming gently, and glancing from time to time at his watch on the table before him; Yves sitting in clenched silence, liberally anathematizing to himself American idiom, French traffic, and his mother's feckless second child.

Conspiracy clearly agreed with Jean-Jacques. His face, as he approached the table, was flushed with an almost sexual excitement; his bearing so studiedly nonchalant that Fredericks feared that an inadvertent car backfire might cause him to drop instantly dead.

"Everything in order?" Fredericks asked as Jean-Jacques reached the table.

"Yes," Jean-Jacques said shrilly, the stress of the three-block walk having raised his voice a clear octave.

"How much?" Fredericks asked.

"Eight hundred and seventy-five thousand francs," he whispered.

"Good." Fredericks extended his hand.

Jean-Jacques gave him the briefcase and began to pull out his chair.

"Don't bother to sit down, Pumpkie," Fredericks said, "this's where you leave."

Yves Cassin slowly looked up at Jean-Jacques.

"'Pumpkie'," he finally said. "It's because of the head?"

When neither Fredericks nor Jean-Jacques responded, Yves began to laugh, softly at first, then more uncontrollably.

"I'm sorry," Fredericks said, with genuine apology, "I forgot."

Mustering those shreds of dignity that remained, Jean-Jacques Cassin straightened his back, turned on his heel, and strode haughtily away, his brother's dry cackle following him.

Ten minutes later, with fully three minutes to spare on Fredericks's deadline, Stuarti arrived.

He was wheeled into the bar by Phillipe, Cassin's adjutant whom Fredericks recalled from his interrogation. If the man felt any large surprise at seeing Fredericks seated with his chief over cocktails in the garden bar of the Intercontinental, his face did not betray it.

"Thank you, Phillipe," Cassin said. "Please wait in the car."

Slumped in the wheelchair, Stuarti was less impassive. His eyes were unnaturally bright, darting about like those of a subterranean animal suddenly and disagreeably surprised in the light. Wheeled to the table, he glanced first at Fredericks, then at Cassin, then again at Fredericks, seeking clues.

"Hello, dear boy," he said cautiously. "Long time, no see."

"It's all right, Mary," Fredericks said. "I'm driving."

"Yes?" Stuarti said carefully.

"Yes," Fredericks said.

Stuarti turned his head to Cassin. "If my tennis game doesn't come back," he said, "I'm suing, you prick."

Cassin looked at him, then looked away.

"Why, dear *boy*," Stuarti exclaimed delightedly, "you *are* driving!"

"You all right, Mary?" Fredericks asked.

"Got me," Stuarti said. "They just filled one arm with Demerol and the other with speed. Right now I feel like an alligator. What're we drinking?"

"I'm not sure you should have anything, Mary," Fredericks said.

Stuarti's hand snaked out and grabbed Fredericks's glass.

"Old enough to be your grandfather," he muttered, draining it. "Let's get some ice cream, shall we?"

"Mr. Fredericks," Cassin interrupted, "you don't actually believe that you'll be able to leave the country, do you?"

"I'm not leaving the country," Fredericks said.

"Oh?" A shadow of disquiet crossed Cassin's face.

Fredericks began to hum, a soft and amelodic hum that was barely audible.

Ignoring Cassin, Stuarti looked at Fredericks carefully for a long moment. When he spoke, his voice was uneasy.

"Why, you're sick, dear boy," he said, "you're sweating."

Cassin cleared his throat, tented his fingers, and again spoke to Fredericks.

"May I ask, then, Mr. Fredericks, what your plans *are?*"

"No," Fredericks said.

"I ask," Cassin continued smoothly, "because while it is clear that you possess rather unique skills, one imagines that it might, just now, be difficult to find an employ which would grant them full exercise...."

"Mr. Fredericks is ill," Stuarti said firmly. "He's suffering from a touch of unrequited loyalty. He needs rest."

"It would be a great shame," Cassin said, "to allow such skills to go to waste...."

"I forbid you to continue this conversation!" Stuarti interrupted. "Mr. Fredericks is..."

"Mr. Fredericks is a killer," Cassin said.

"No!" Stuarti cried. "To be impelled by conscience to pursue objectives which can only be attained through means which conscience finds abhorrent is the modern condition! It's *obscene* to suggest..."

"Are you offering me a job?" Fredericks asked.

"Yes," Cassin said.

Fredericks's hand slid gently to the side of Cassin's neck, his eyes seemed momentarily to cloud, and suddenly the three of them were very much alone, despite the crowd around them.

"*No,*" Stuarti said firmly.

It was not clear how long the tension endured, but when Phillipe, Cassin's adjutant, spoke, both Cassin and Stuarti were startled, for they had not noticed his approach.

"They want to speak to you," he said, addressing Cassin.

"Tell them I'll call back," Cassin said, his voice strained.

"They don't want to speak to you on the phone."

"Then tell them it'll have to be later," Cassin said.

"They said *now,*" Phillipe said, and though he remained expressionless, his address was no longer that of acolyte to Cassin's high priest.

Fredericks's hand slipped from Cassin's neck as he stood.

"Goodbye, Colonel Laloux," he said.

He did not look back as he wheeled Stuarti from the room.

They emerged from the hotel into warm, late-afternoon sunshine in the rue Castiglione. A block away, early rush-hour traffic was already thickening in the rue de Rivoli.

"*Now* can we get some ice cream?" Stuarti asked. "Speed always gives me a powerful craving for butter-almond."

"You're going home, Mary," Fredericks said, "and take a nap like the other oldsters. If the traffic's not too bad on the *quais* and you don't get stuck in the rue des Saints-Pères, you still might be able to catch *'Monde des Animaux, Monde des Plantes'*."

"'Oldster'?" Stuarti said. "Who're you calling an 'oldster'?"

The chauffeur of the lead taxi in the rank emerged from his cab, his face darkening at the sight of Stuarti's wheelchair. The hundred-franc note that Fredericks handed him, however, transformed his swelling indignation to the purest solicitude.

"The place de Furstemberg," Fredericks said. "The gentleman will need help with some steps when you get there."

"But certainly," the driver said. "A pleasure."

"'Oldster'!" sniffed Stuarti. "Listen, there was a picture of David Eisenhower in last week's *Newsweek*. Fucker's bald, looks like somebody's grandfather. Doesn't look like Howdy Doody at *all* anymore...."

Fredericks lifted Stuarti from the wheelchair as easily as though he were a child and placed him gently in the back seat of the cab.

"...I mean," Stuarti continued, "you're not exactly a *rookie* yourself, dear boy."

Smiling, Fredericks closed the door. Through the open window he handed Stuarti the briefcase.

"Good news, Mary," he said. "Your pension came through."

His face suddenly very serious, Stuarti looked at Fredericks for a long moment. He began to speak, but Fredericks shook his head.

"Well," Stuarti said finally, "I suppose it's nice to know that the system works."

"Yes," Fredericks said.

"You *are* all right, dear boy?" Stuarti said, an edge of anxiety to his voice. "Not suffering from hardening of the categories or anything?"

"Goodbye, Mary," Fredericks said.

"I mean, you *do* have plans, dear boy?" Stuarti pressed. "It's over, after all."

"Sure," Fredericks said, and again the soft humming came.

"A wife and nippers, maybe?" Stuarti continued bravely, his voice cracking slightly. "Just the ticket, I hear. Change some diapers, forget about the world."

"That's it," Fredericks said.

"Pleased to hear it, dear boy." Stuarti controlled his voice with difficulty. "You won't forget to send snaps?"

Still looking at Stuarti, Fredericks slapped the roof of the cab. The car pulled rapidly away, caught the yellow light at the corner, turned into the rue de Rivoli, and was gone.

TWENTY ONE

IT WAS FIVE o'clock that afternoon when Winthrop Burnham, having finished his banking, emerged from the stately double doors of Handelsbank N.W. into Zurich's Paradplatz and the cool air of early evening.

The sidewalks about him thronged with home-going Zurichers; chunky in contour, bourgeois in frontage, their faces set in that stolid incuriosity particular to the Swiss.

The stress of servicing the accounts—and the numbing awareness of the personal defeat it represented—had drained him, and as he stood on the curb and breathed deeply he noticed that his legs were trembling.

In a café on the Banhofstrasse Burnham had a coffee and two cognacs, calming himself and allowing the rush-hour crowds to thin before returning to the hotel. When again he emerged into the street, the evening was thickening and there was a chill in the now nearly deserted streets.

As he walked slowly along the Limatstrasse, Burnham became aware of a car idling softly along behind him in the gutter. He turned his head and was reassured to see that it was only a taxi. Looking more closely, Burnham noticed that there appeared to be someone in the rear seat of the taxi, and as the car pulled level with him and the passenger's window was lowered, he wondered whether he was to be offered a whore or advantageous exchange rates.

From the rear seat a voice with a thick Slavic accent said softly, "Gospodin Lèon?"

"No, thank you," Burnham said in firm school-boy German, "I don't want any."

The silenced discharge of the heavy pistol was no louder than a cough. The bullet blew Burnham's chest apart.

The taxi slowly gathered speed and then, red tail lights winking in the gathering dark, was gone.

Up the river, far beyond the head of the lake, snowy mountains gleamed, impossibly white.

It was dusk when Fredericks emerged from the Tuileries. The shadows beneath the chestnut trees were blackening, and the sky above, its low clouds smoky purple, was rapidly deepening to night.

He called Danielle from a public telephone in the place du Palais Royal.

He was not sure why he was calling, and thus, when she answered, she had to say hello twice before he spoke.

"Hello, Dany," he said.

"Noah?" she said. "Noah, is that you!?"

"Yes," Fredericks said.

"Noah, where are you?"

"Are you all right?" Fredericks asked.

"Are you in France?" she said, ignoring his question.

"Yes."

"Are you in Paris?"

"Yes."

"Can I come to you? Just tell me...."

"No," Fredericks said.

"Then come to me," Danielle said. "Can you come to me?"

"I don't know," Fredericks said. "Maybe later."

"Noah, listen to me," Danielle said, her voice urgent. "Whatever it is, it's all right. It doesn't matter. But come *now....*"

"It's not *quite* all right yet...." Fredericks said, and then stopped speaking as he was shaken by a brief spasm of nausea which he supposed to be hunger.

"Oh, God, Noah, come now," Danielle said, her voice beginning to break. "If you don't come now you won't come, I *know* it! Listen, I know you hate the Mètro, but you don't have to take the Mètro, or a cab, or anything. Just walk, Noah. You like to walk. Walk here to me."

"Maybe later," Fredericks said.

Danielle began to weep, helplessly. "Oh, Noah," she said, "you're hurt, I know you're hurt. Please come to me, come now, come now...."

This she repeated several times, weeping, even though she knew that Fredericks was no longer on the line.

Fredericks left the public telephone, walking west on the rue de Rivoli. His mind, as he walked, was empty, weatherless. He was aware, as he had been in Burnham's street, of a slight sensation of deafness, as though he were separated from the world by glass.

It was only when he turned into the rue du Marché Saint-Honoré that he realized again where he was, and why.

Looking up at the street sign, he smiled.

There was an odd quality to the smile, a quality of something secretly fractured but finely joined; the smile, perhaps, of someone who, despite the evidence of sweetest air and softest cloud, knows that it will be winter soon.

At 11:30 that night, truncating his shift by thirty minutes as was his habit, Inspecteur Principal Michel Bourrelier emerged from the doors of the Troisième Brigade Territoriale into the empty place du Marché Saint-Honoré.

He had been brought, that afternoon, two suspects for interrogation—a Dutch girl and her boyfriend accused of possession of hashish—and although the girl's weeping had given him a slight headache, the evening had been a diverting one.

The night air was thick and chill, promising rain, and the Inspecteur paused on the curb to zip the old cardigan that he wore underneath his suit over his heavy paunch.

Picking up his briefcase, he crossed the deserted place and entered the empty and shadowed rue Gomboust.

The officers' parking lot was in a dark and narrow *ruelle* giving off to the left, midway down the street. As he reached the mouth of the alley and started to enter, he stopped abruptly, suddenly alert.

He was not sure what he had heard. It had sounded like humming; not a tune, exactly, but a soft and amelodic humming, and as he peered into the darkness, his eyes straining, it seemed as though a large shape in the shadows shifted once, slightly, and was still.

"Qui est là?" he called, his throat tightening.

When there was no response, he placed his briefcase at his feet and opened it. From it he withdrew a flashlight.

262

"Who's there?" he repeated, playing its weak beam over and beneath the cars.

Nothing.

When the light reached the wall where he thought he had seen movement, there was only a deserted doorway, the night dew dark on the ancient stone.

After a moment he extinguished the flashlight, replaced it in his briefcase, and breathed deeply.

Child of Descartes, his comfort lay in Logic. The humming sound, he explained to himself with firm sympathy, was simply the product of overwork and the damned girl's noise; the illusion of motion he dismissed, after a moment's thought, as a common phenomenon of uncertain light.

Darkness conquered, mind triumphant, he smiled to himself with understandable pride, picked up his briefcase, and entered the alley-mouth.

The force with which his shoulders struck the cobblestones drove the breath entirely from his body and jarred the dentures from his mouth.

The iron hand on his throat and the knee driven into his chest pinned him to the ground as helplessly as a lepidopterist's specimen.

The shape above him was motionless and silent, the stillness nearly that of prayer. As Bourrelier's vision returned, the heavy clouds above parted briefly, and with horror he recognized Fredericks's face. Fredericks's eyes, even in the dim moonlight, were of spectral blue, the color of poisonous night-flowers, and held Bourrelier in an abstracted stare, a gaze from the silent zone of the brain that seemed to see not his face, but rather only the skull beneath the skin.

Fredericks's free hand moved slowly before

Bourrelier's face, and with a soft click the oiled tongue of a switchblade knife blossomed from his hand, gleaming.

"It's not the *same* knife you were looking for," Fredericks said softly, "but it's the same *sort* of knife."

Time passed without measure, and it was only when next the low clouds broke that Fredericks spoke again, this time in English, which Bourrelier could not understand.

"I can't stay," Fredericks said, as though in apology to a host. "I've got somewhere else to go."

His arm rose, and the glittering blade descended, drawn down in a terrible curve, and as Bourrelier's body twisted futilely, Fredericks drove the knife into a crack between two cobblestones next to his ear, snapping the blade off at the haft.

His vision swimming black as his lungs sobbed in air, Bourrelier could not see Fredericks leave, nor could he move, as though Death still inhabited the space where Fredericks had been.

All he could hear was the receding sound of Fredericks's footsteps: tentative at first, like a man entering a newly opened room of the world, then steadier and stronger, heading home.